Usborne
Illustrated
Arabian
Nights

Anna Milbourne

Illustrated by Alida Massari

Designed by Sam Chandler

Contents

Usborne
Illustrated

Arabian Nights

Legend has it that long ago, in the lands of Arabia, there lived a clever and beautiful woman named Sheherazade who, for a thousand and one nights, told such good stories they saved her life.

They have come to be known as...

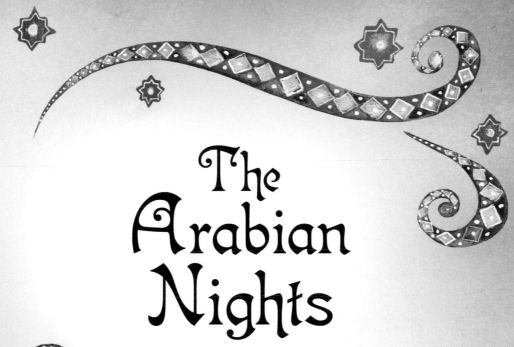

The Arabian Nights

nce upon a time, there lived a hugely rich and powerful sultan. He ruled his country with kindness because he was in love. He and his wife were the happiest couple alive.

Or so he thought…

One day, the sultan returned from a horse ride to find his wife in the arms of another man. The sultan was devastated. His heart was broken. But instead of being sad, the sultan was furious. He had his wife and her lover killed on the spot. "If this woman can fail me, then no woman is to be trusted. I will never love again," he vowed.

What the heartbroken sultan did next was so horrifying it has gone down in history. Every afternoon he married a different woman, only to put her to death the following morning.

His kingdom quaked under his fearful reign. Parents hid their daughters away so they wouldn't be forced to marry the sultan. Girls fled the country. Newborn baby girls were met with sorrow instead of joy, since nobody knew when the sultan's terrible decree would end.

Then one morning, a beautiful young woman named Sheherazade said to her father, "I'm going to volunteer to marry the sultan next."

Her father's eyes filled with tears. "Why would you do such a thing? You are far too good and far too clever to throw your life away."

"Trust me, Father," said Sheherazade. "I have a plan that might save me, and anyone else, from having to die at the sultan's hand."

Reluctantly, her father let her go.

The sultan welcomed the girl's proposal, and married her that very day. In the evening as they were getting ready to go to sleep, Sheherazade said to the sultan, "The night is long and I'm not sure I can sleep, knowing I will die tomorrow... To while away the time, may I tell you a story?"

"Very well," said the sultan.

And so,
when the sultan was settled in his bed,
Sheherazade began…

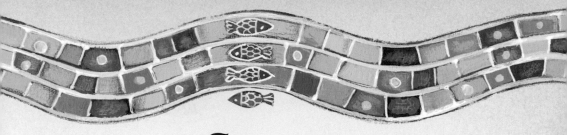

The
Fisherman
and the Genie

There was once a poor fisherman who lived on whatever he caught from the sea. Most days he caught a fish or two for his supper, but some days he went hungry.

One morning, he went down to the sea as usual and cast his net. When he pulled on it, the net was surprisingly heavy.

"I must have caught lots of fish," he thought gleefully, as he heaved his catch on to the shore. But all he'd caught was a big old cart wheel.

Shaking his head, the fisherman untangled his net and cast it further out to sea. This time, when he pulled on it, the net was so heavy it hardly moved. "This could be hundreds of fish," he thought eagerly, as he bent double and hauled his catch on to the shore. But this time all he'd caught was a pile of broken clay pots.

Rolling his eyes, the fisherman untangled his net and cast it even further out to sea. When he pulled on it, the net was so heavy it didn't move an inch. "It's as heavy as a thousand fish," he thought hopefully. He tugged with all his might, and eventually pulled it to shore. But this time he'd caught a load of rocks.

The fisherman sighed. "I've only got time to cast my net once more today. If I don't find anything, I'll have nothing for supper," he said. He untangled his net and cast it out as far as he possibly could into the sea. "Please let me catch something amazing this time," he prayed.

Suddenly the line went taut. When the fisherman pulled on it, the net was so heavy that he couldn't move it no matter how hard he pulled. So he tied it to a stake on the beach, and waded into the water to try to land his catch.

He pushed and pulled, and heaved and shoved, and eventually managed to get the net to shore. But he was disappointed to find he hadn't caught a single fish. Instead, he had dragged up a large copper bottle, which was sealed with a cork.

"I still don't have a morsel to eat, but a copper bottle must be worth something," the fisherman said. He rubbed the bottle until it gleamed. "I'll sell it in the market and buy some food."

He untangled his net and started trying to drag the bottle up the beach, but it was too heavy for him. "Maybe it's full of sea water," the fisherman thought, and he pulled out the cork to empty the bottle.

No sooner had he opened it than a column of blue smoke billowed out into the sky.

The fisherman staggered back in shock as the smoke gathered into a giant cloud above him, and took the shape of a towering figure. It was a genie! "Who dares release me?" thundered the genie.

The Fisherman and the Genie

His mouth was cavernous and his voice made the very earth tremble.

"It was me," squeaked the fisherman. The genie glared down at the terrified man. "Get ready to die," he said.

"You ungrateful thing," the fisherman protested, suddenly filled with indignation. "What did I do to deserve that?"

The genie shrugged. "Years ago, when I tried to kill King Solomon, he ordered some other genies to imprison me in this bottle and throw the bottle into the sea. At first I said to myself, 'I will give all the gold inside the earth to the one who sets me free.'"

"That would have been a fine catch," said the fisherman.

The genie continued, "After a hundred years,

I said to myself, 'I will give all the jewels inside the earth as well as all its gold to the one who sets me free.'"

"That would have been a wonderful catch," sighed the fisherman.

The genie continued, "After another hundred years, I thought to myself, 'Whoever comes and sets me free now has taken so long about it that he doesn't deserve to live. I'll kill him, whoever he is.' So there you have it. Now choose how you want to die."

The fisherman's mind raced as he tried to think of a way to escape death. "I'm not strong enough to fight a genie," he thought. "But maybe I'm clever enough to outwit one." He looked the genie up and down and declared, "I don't believe you can kill me."

"WHAT?" spluttered the genie.

"You're a liar," said the fisherman scornfully. "I don't believe you could have come from inside that bottle. You're far too big."

"I'm a GENIE, you fool," he bellowed, turning purple with indignation. "I have magical powers. I can do anything I like! Of COURSE I can fit into that bottle."

The fisherman shook his head. "No way," he said. He picked up the bottle and the cork, and he waved them at the genie. "Your big toe wouldn't even fit inside here. You're not powerful enough to change that."

"I am!" insisted the genie. "I can make myself as big as the sky or as small as a beetle. I'm certainly powerful enough to fit inside a silly bottle."

The fisherman snorted. "I won't believe it unless I see it with my own eyes," he said.

"Then watch this!" roared the genie, and he disappeared down the neck of the bottle. "Do you believe me NOW?" his voice echoed out.

In the blink of an eye the fisherman pushed the stopper back into the top of the bottle. "Yes, I do," he laughed. "You fit very nicely, thank you."

"Oh no!" wailed the genie. "Let me out, please."

"Not likely," said the fisherman. "I'm throwing you right back into the sea."

"Please, please," begged the genie. "I'll make you rich to the end of your days."

The fisherman paused. "And you'll promise to leave me alone and never cross my path again?" he said.

"I promise," whimpered the genie.
So the fisherman pulled the cork out of the bottle. He gulped nervously as the genie billowed out again and loomed above him.

But then the genie bowed down low and stretched out his hand. "Come," he said.

The fisherman stepped onto the enormous, outstretched palm, and the genie lifted him high into the air. "See that lake?" he said, pointing down into the forest. A lake gleamed silver among the trees.

"I see it," said the fisherman.

"Nobody knows of its existence but me – and now you," said the genie. "It's a magic lake with

fish in it, the likes of which you've never seen.
Throw your net in and you'll catch four fish:
one red, one blue, one yellow, one white. If you
take them to the sultan, he will reward you with
riches beyond your wildest dreams."

The genie lowered the fisherman gently
back down onto the beach. After bowing to
the fisherman once more, he flew away across
the sea.

The fisherman hurried off to the lake.
When he got there, he cast his net into the
water and pulled it out again. Just as the genie had
promised, he had caught four fish – one red,
one blue, one yellow, and one white – each more
beautiful than the last.

He took them to the sultan, who was
delighted. "These are the most splendid fish
I've ever seen!" he exclaimed. He was so pleased
with the present, that he gave the fisherman
enough gold to make him rich to the end of
his days.

After that, the fisherman lived very happily
indeed. He got married and had a family. He
continued fishing in his spare time and enjoyed
telling his children and grandchildren all about
the time he had met a genie.

Once, later in his life, he tried to show his children the magical lake so they could fish there too. But it was nowhere to be found.

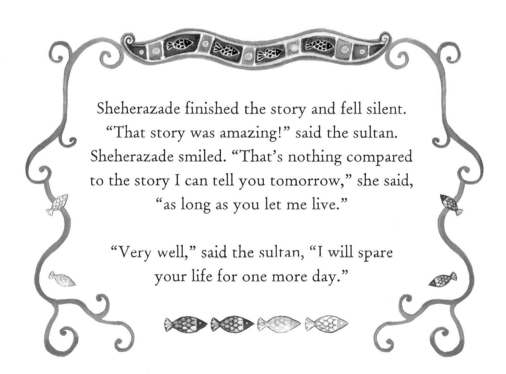

Sheherazade finished the story and fell silent. "That story was amazing!" said the sultan. Sheherazade smiled. "That's nothing compared to the story I can tell you tomorrow," she said, "as long as you let me live."

"Very well," said the sultan, "I will spare your life for one more day."

The next night,
when the sultan was settled in his bed,
Sheherazade began...

Ali Baba
and the
Forty Thieves

Chop, chop, chop. Ali Baba was hard at work in the forest cutting up wood to sell. He was just loading the logs onto his donkey's back when he heard a rumble of hooves. "That sounds like an awful lot of horses," he thought.

When the distant rumble grew to a roar,
Ali Baba climbed up a tree to hide. His donkey
had just wandered out of sight when a group of
men on horseback galloped into view. They
stopped under the tree where Ali Baba was hiding.

The men were scarred and mean-looking,
and they each carried a bulging sack. "Thieves,"
thought Ali Baba. He counted them quickly –
there were forty. Terrified, he held his breath so
he wouldn't make a sound.

The biggest, toughest-looking thief jumped
off his horse, glanced around him, then pushed
through the bushes surrounding a large rock. Ali
Baba was surprised to see a door.

"Open Sesame!" commanded the thief. With a
grinding noise, the door slid open.

The thief went inside, followed by the others.

The last to pass through the door said, "Close Sesame!" and the rock door slid shut.

An unbearable amount of time passed, and Ali Baba stayed up the tree, not daring to move. Then, he heard a man shout, "Open Sesame!" from inside the rock. All forty thieves came out again. After shutting the door with, "Close Sesame!", they mounted their horses and rode off.

Shakily, Ali Baba climbed back down the tree. He was frightened, but he was curious too. So he pushed his way through the bushes to the door and whispered timidly, "Open Sesame." To his delight, the door opened.

He stepped inside to find a large, bright cavern full of glowing treasure. There were piles of gold coins, heaps of costly silks, strings of pearls, ruby rings and chests spilling over with diamonds.

Ali Baba could scarcely believe his eyes. "I bet they wouldn't miss a sack or two of gold..." he thought. He picked up two sacks the thieves had left behind, filled them with gold coins, and hurried out of the cave. "Close Sesame," he commanded, and the door slid shut behind him.

Ali Baba found his donkey and strapped the sacks onto its back. He covered them with firewood, and led his donkey home.

When he showed his wife the gold, she gasped in horror. "What are you doing with all that? Did you do something bad to get it?" she asked.

Ali Baba told her the whole story. "But we have to keep it a secret," he said. "If the thieves ever heard about it, I'm sure they'd find me and kill me on the spot."

"Let's just spend it quickly," said his wife.

"No, no," said Ali Baba. "Everyone knows we barely have two coins to rub together. We'll bury it in the backyard."

"Can't we give our son some?" pleaded his wife. "He could use it to set up a shop."

"Not yet," insisted Ali Baba. "It will only draw people's attention to us."

While he was busy digging a hole in the backyard, his wife tried to count the gold. But there was too much to count, so she hurried off to her sister-in-law's house to  borrow the bushel basket she used for measuring large quantities of grain.

Ali Baba's brother, Kasim, and his wife were

very rich, but they never gave a penny to Ali Baba and his wife. In fact, they looked down their noses at them for being so poor.

When Ali Baba's wife arrived asking to borrow a measuring basket, Kasim's wife was curious. "Whatever can *she* have that she needs to measure in my basket?" she wondered.

Rather than simply asking, she secretly smeared soft candle wax in the bottom of the basket before handing it over. "Whatever she's measuring will stick to the wax," she thought with satisfaction.

None the wiser, Ali Baba's wife thanked her and ran home to measure how many basketfuls of gold they had. Then she returned the basket.

When Kasim's wife looked inside, she found a gold coin stuck to the bottom. "Since when did *they* have any gold?" she gasped.

When she told Kasim, he marched straight to Ali Baba's house. "Where did you get gold?" he demanded on the doorstep.

Ali Baba ushered him inside, saying, "Hush, brother. I don't want the whole town to know!" Since he was an honest man, he told his brother everything. "The thieves will kill me if they find out, so please keep it a secret," he finished.

"I want some gold too," Kasim insisted. "Tell me how to get it or I'll let your secret out."

So Ali Baba told his brother how to find the cave, and gave him the magic words to open the door. "Be careful they don't find you," he urged.

"Of course not!" snorted Kasim, and he strutted away without so much as a 'thank you'.

The next day, Kasim took ten donkeys into the forest. He tied them to a tree, pushed through the bushes and shouted, "Open Sesame!"

The door slid open, revealing the cavern full of treasure. "Close Sesame!" said Kasim as he rushed inside. Chuckling to himself in glee, he began to fill the twenty sacks he'd brought. He poured chests of coins into them, and stuffed them with fistfuls of ruby bracelets, armfuls of emerald necklaces, and mounds and mounds of diamonds. Then he staggered to the door. "Open up!" he said. But the door remained closed.

Kasim's face fell. In his whirl of greed, he had forgotten the magic words. He scratched his head. "Um... Open Barley!" he shouted.

The door stayed put.

"Open Corn!" yelled Kasim. "Open Wheat! Open Rice! Open Chickpea!"

The door didn't move an inch.

Suddenly he heard the rumble of hooves. The thieves were coming back! Before Kasim could even think of hiding, a gruff voice shouted, "What are these donkeys doing here? Someone must be inside. Open Sesame!"

The door slid open, and he found himself face-to-face with forty angry thieves.

The thieves killed Kasim on the spot. When Ali Baba crept into the forest the following night to find out what had happened to his brother, he found Kasim's body outside the door of the cave.

Sadly, he took his dead brother home. Kasim's wife was distraught when she learned what had happened. "But the worst thing is," Ali Baba said, "you can't mourn him until we've convinced people that he died some other way."

"What on earth are we supposed to tell them?" she wailed.

"I think maybe Marjana could help," said Ali Baba thoughtfully. Marjana was a servant girl in Kasim's household. Ali Baba thought she was both clever and loyal. So they told the girl everything. "Can we count on your help?" Ali Baba asked her.

Marjana nodded. "Tomorrow, I will go and buy medicine, and say my master is very sick," she suggested. "The next day, I'll say he is even sicker. On the third day, we can tell everyone he has died and it won't seem as suspicious."

So that's just what they did. Marjana played her part very well, and on the third day, when Kasim's wife was allowed to wail about the loss of her husband in public, the whole town was convinced he had died of an incurable disease. The funeral took place, and Kasim was buried without any suspicion.

The day after Kasim's funeral, his widow asked Ali Baba and his wife to come and live with her. "I can't bear to live on my own," she said.

Ali Baba and his wife agreed. They dug up the gold from their backyard and took it with them. "This belongs to all of us now," Ali Baba told his sister-in-law. "But we mustn't spend a penny yet, as the thieves will be looking for us."

"Don't worry," said Kasim's widow, locking the gold in a large wooden chest in the storeroom. "It will be perfectly safe here."

Kasim had owned a shop selling rugs in the town, which his wife now gave to Ali Baba's son. He was delighted, and worked hard to make a success of it.

Meanwhile, in the woods, the thieves were forming a plan. "The man we found in our lair knew about the treasure, which means other people probably know too," said the head thief. "We must find anyone else who knows our secret and kill them. I want you to split up and search all the nearby towns for clues."

So the thieves did just that. They hung around towns, watching and chatting with people. Each night they reported back to their leader.

Despite Ali Baba's warnings not to spend the gold, Kasim's widow started to take a little every day to buy herself treats. "My husband is dead and gone. I deserve something to cheer me up," she thought. Every day she came home with something new – necklaces and clothes, a haircut and painted nails, cakes and expensive perfume.

In the bustling marketplace, she didn't notice that a stranger was watching her. He was there every day, sitting in a café or loitering in the square and eyeing her as she spent more and more gold pieces buying pretty things.

"Someone's spending money like water," he commented to the vegetable seller one afternoon.

The man tutted and shook his head. "That's Kasim's widow," he said. "He died very suddenly. One day we saw him in his shop, right as rain, the next he was gone. Perhaps she's still in shock."

"Poor thing," said the stranger. He slipped away through the crowds and followed her home.

The next evening, Ali Baba heard a tap on the front door of his new home. He opened it to find a merchant standing by a cart which was loaded with forty enormous jars.

"Good evening," said the merchant. "I have come to sell my oil in the market tomorrow, but I have nowhere to stay. I wondered… Would you be so good as to give me a quiet corner to lay my head for the night?"

Ali Baba welcomed the merchant in. "Drive

your cart into the courtyard and I'll show you to your room," he said warmly.

He didn't notice the man's sly grin, nor did he see him whisper something to the jars before leaving them in the courtyard for the night.

But the servant girl Marjana did. She was suspicious, and decided to keep watch to make sure no harm would come to the family.

When everyone else had gone to bed, Marjana sat at the kitchen window. After a few hours, her oil lamp burned down and went out. "If I go into the cellar to get more oil, I may miss something," she thought. "So I'll just take a little from the merchant's oil jars." She crept over to the cart.

As she neared the first jar, a man's voice whispered. "Is it time?"

Marjana's blood ran cold with fear.

Anyone less brave would have panicked to hear the unexpected voice. But not Marjana. In the lowest voice she could manage, she answered, "Not yet but soon."

She walked past the second jar and another man's voice asked, "Is it time?"

"Not yet but soon," Marjana answered again.

She gave the same answer to all thirty-nine jars. When she came to the last one, it remained silent. Peering in the top, she found it full of oil, so she filled her oil jug and walked away.

In the kitchen, she lit her oil lamp. As the wavering golden flame surged up, she tried to think what she should do. How could she save the household? They would be murdered in their beds if she didn't do something. Slowly a plan came to her.

She lit a fire and put a huge cooking pot on it. Then, making many journeys to and from the cart, she filled the pot with oil, which she heated on the fire.

When the oil was boiling hot, she scooped up a jugful, then hurried over to the jars. She poured the oil into the first jar and sealed the lid. Back and forth, she did the same to all the other jars, and each thief was killed where he hid.

After she had put out the fire, and washed the jug and the cooking pot clean, Marjana went to get ready for bed.

In the dead of night the visitor, who was of course the head thief, went downstairs and tapped on the jars. "It's time," he hissed. "Come out and murder this family."

But from the jars came no reply.

The thief pulled the stopper out of the first jar and found a dead man inside. He looked inside each of the others and was horrified to find that his entire band of thieves was dead.

Marjana was watching from the window as the visitor vaulted over the garden wall and escaped. Then she climbed into bed and went to sleep.

The next day, Ali Baba left early and returned much later for supper. When he came in, he asked Marjana, "Why didn't the merchant take his oil to market?"

"Because he wasn't a merchant, and they weren't jars of oil," Marjana replied coolly as she served the meal. "There were forty thieves here last night, planning to kill you in your beds."

The two other women squealed in horror.

"And now?" said Ali Baba.

"There are thirty-nine dead thieves in those jars over there. Their leader climbed over the wall late last night," said Marjana. "Now eat up your supper before it gets cold."

They had no choice but to bury the thieves in the garden, but after that horrible task, life went back to normal. Kasim's widow stopped spending the gold, and they lived a quiet life, hoping the thief would never come back.

But deep in the forest, hidden in his lair, the thief was plotting his revenge. Furious with Ali Baba's family for ruining his plan, he couldn't bear to leave them in peace. So he lay low, and waited for his chance...

In the town, Ali Baba's son was making a great success of his uncle's rug shop. Kasim had been known as a ruthless and greedy businessman, but

Ali Baba's son was generous and fair, and was soon well-liked among all the traders. The business flourished, and he was happy.

One day, a new trader opened a shop next to his, selling trinkets and household wares. He invited Ali Baba's son for tea, and took him out for a lavish lunch. The two chatted, and soon became friends.

Ali Baba's son wanted to invite his new friend home for dinner. But his own lodgings were very small, so he asked his father if he could bring the tradesman to his house.

"Of course," said Ali Baba. "Why don't you both come this evening? I'll ask Marjana to make something special."

When his son arrived with the guest that evening, Ali Baba welcomed them in. They drank iced tea together and chatted until Marjana was ready to serve dinner.

Marjana brought dishes of fragrant stew and placed them on the table. When she saw the guest, shivers ran down her spine. The man had disguised himself, with a large, bushy beard and different clothes, but she would have recognized him anywhere. It was the head thief.

She watched him carefully as she served the food. As he reached forward to pick up his drink, she glimpsed a dagger tucked inside his robe. Marjana said nothing, but finished serving and returned to the kitchen.

Ali Baba didn't suspect a thing, and chatted happily to his guest. When they had finished eating, he was surprised to see Marjana enter the room with two musicians.

Marjana was wearing wide pantaloons that gathered around her ankles. She had shining bangles on her arms, and carried a scarf with coins sewn along the edge. "Would you like me to dance for you?" she asked.

Ali Baba looked at his guest, who nodded eagerly and sat back to watch. The musicians began to play a rhythmic tune, and Marjana started to dance.

She swayed to and fro, moving her hands gracefully, like a tree bending in the wind. She rose up on her toes and spun very slowly, looking back at the guest. She wrapped the scarf around herself, and whirled it away again prettily.

As she turned, Ali Baba's son noticed a glint of silver in her hand. When she lifted the scarf above her head, he saw that it was a silver dagger. He had known Marjana for years, and trusted her absolutely, so it didn't occur to him to do anything to stop her, but his mind was awash with confusion.

Marjana began to spin around again. She spun faster and faster and faster, until she was a blur. Then suddenly she lunged at the guest and stabbed him right through the heart. The head thief gasped in shock, and slumped down dead.

There was a stunned silence. Marjana sat down, breathing hard. "Look inside his robes," she told a speechless Ali Baba.

Doing as she said, Ali Baba found the large dagger hidden in the man's clothing. "But why?

How? Who?" he began.

"Look closely at his face," Marjana urged him. "Don't you recognize him?"

Finally, Ali Baba realized who the man was. "You have saved our lives for the second time, Marjana," he said. "How can we ever thank you?"

"It's what anyone would do," Marjana replied.

"No," said Ali Baba's son. "Only someone as clever and brave as you could do something like this. Without you we would all be in trouble."

"You're far too clever to be a servant," said Ali Baba, "Suppose I give you a share of the gold, and your freedom as a reward?"

"I don't think I can bear to lose you from our family," Ali Baba's son said a little shyly. "I wonder… will you marry me?"

Marjana took his hand. "I'd love to," she said.

After several years had passed, Ali Baba went
back to the thieves' secret lair. The treasure was
still there, gathering dust, so he took the rest of it
and shared it with the people of his town.
He and his family lived happily until the end
of their days.

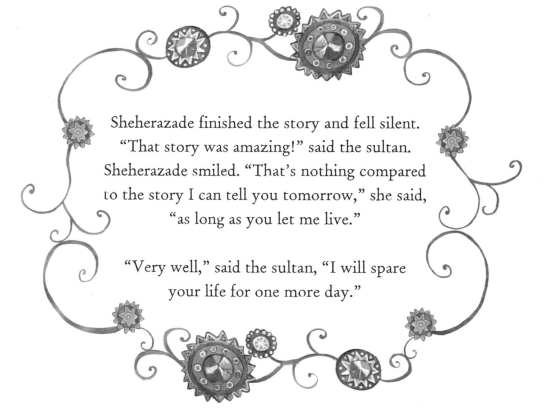

Sheherazade finished the story and fell silent.
"That story was amazing!" said the sultan.
Sheherazade smiled. "That's nothing compared
to the story I can tell you tomorrow," she said,
"as long as you let me live."

"Very well," said the sultan, "I will spare
your life for one more day."

The next night,
when the sultan was settled in his bed,
Sheherazade began...

The Sultan and the Doctor

Yunan the Magnificent had everything he could possibly want. He was the sultan of a magnificent land, who lived in a magnificent palace and was served by a magnificent army. Almost everything was magnificent. Everything, that is, except for his health.

He suffered from a terrible disease called leprosy, which gave him painful sores all over his skin. Doctor after doctor had tried, but completely failed, to cure him. "I feel anything *but* magnificent," he used to say.

One day, a new doctor came to see the sultan. "I have come to cure you," he announced.

The sultan waved him away. "Every doctor in the land has tried," he said. "They have already tried every lotion…"

"I won't use a lotion," the doctor interrupted.

"They have already tried every potion…" the sultan continued.

"I won't use a potion," the doctor interrupted again.

"They have already tried every ointment…" the sultan insisted.

"I won't use an ointment," the doctor interrupted for a third time.

The sultan looked at him with interest. "What else is there?" he asked.

"If you play polo this afternoon with the polo stick I give you, then have a bath and go to bed, in the morning you will be cured," the doctor said.

"Really?" said the sultan, his eyes lighting up with hope.

"Really," replied the doctor.

In a private room, the doctor began to work. He unpacked glass vials and strange herbs, and he ground up spices and mixed them with unusual-smelling liquids. By noon the medicine was ready.

From one of his bags, he took out a polo stick, which was hollow in the middle. He unscrewed the top and poured the mixture inside the stick.

Then he presented the polo stick to the sultan. "Here it is, Your Highness. Have a good game."

That afternoon, the doctor and all the courtiers gathered around the polo field to watch. The sultan rode out on his horse and began the game, hitting the ball way up into the air. The polo players galloped around the field, fighting for the ball. One of them managed to hit it and soon they were all racing to the goal. Before long, the sultan was sweaty and breathless.

"Keep going!" called the doctor, so the sultan played on. He swung his polo stick at the ball and urged his horse into a gallop. He scored a spectacular goal and everybody cheered.

After some time, the doctor called, "That's enough! Please go and bathe, then eat something and go to bed right away."

The sultan handed the doctor his polo stick, and went to do as he was told. The doctor unscrewed the polo stick and looked inside. "Good, good," he murmured to himself. All of the mixture had disappeared.

The sultan's vizier, a suspicious man, was eyeing the doctor as he did this. "I am the chief advisor to the sultan," he said. "I demand to know what you put in there!"

"Medicine, which was absorbed by the sultan's hand during the game," the doctor explained. "His activity made the cure circulate around his body. I expect a full recovery."

When the sultan awoke the next morning, he was free from pain for the first time in years. He examined himself in a mirror and found that his skin was smooth, without a trace of leprosy left.

He strode through his palace to the throne room. "I'm cured!" he called out in delight. "Bring me the doctor!"

"How do you feel?" the doctor asked as he was ushered into the room. The sultan engulfed him in a bear hug. "Magnificent," he said. "You will be richly rewarded, my friend. But first, let us celebrate!"

He clapped his hands and servants came running. "Set the tables for a royal feast and tell the musicians to get ready."

Then he turned to his vizier. "Announce to the entire land that today will be a holiday, dedicated to my new royal doctor," he ordered.

The vizier bowed and turned to leave, but threw the doctor a dark glance as he went. He was seething with jealousy.

All that day and all the next, there was feasting and celebration at the palace. The sultan wouldn't be parted from his new friend. He sat by his side talking to him the whole time, he rewarded the doctor with coffers of gold, and he ordered a beautiful house to be built for him.

On the third day, the vizier managed to speak to the sultan alone. "I have some concerns about the doctor," he said.

"Is he alright?" asked the sultan, alarmed.

"Couldn't be better," said the vizier irritably. "But I think he's not all that he seems."

The vizier asked the sultan to walk with him in the gardens. He led the way between the splashing fountains, where his words would not be overheard.

"We don't know where the man came from,"

said the vizier, "and yet he has such great power..."

"Indeed," the sultan beamed. "He healed me!"

"Yes," said the vizier, "but if he can heal you by giving you a polo stick to hold, then he could just as easily kill you by giving you a flower to smell."

The sultan frowned. "What are you saying?"

"We don't know anything about him," said the vizier. "He has gained your trust very quickly and now has the power to do as he pleases!"

The sultan looked uncomfortable. "I suppose that's true," he said.

The vizier seized his chance. "In fact," he said, "it wouldn't surprise me if he had been plotting your downfall all along. Perhaps he works for a rival sultan who wants to conquer our land."

"But he has done nothing but good *so far*," the sultan protested weakly.

"All the more reason to stop him now before he can do any harm," urged the vizier, warming to his purpose. "Do you want to wait until it's too late? You must kill him now before he kills you!" he insisted.

"Wait a minute," said the sultan. "I don't want to find myself in the position of that sultan in the story who kills his falcon, do I?"

"Which story is that?" asked the vizier.

So the sultan began:

There was once a sultan who owned a trusty falcon. He went hunting with it every day. One hot afternoon, he stopped at a cool spring. First he filled his cup and offered his bird some water, but the falcon knocked the cup from his hand.

The sultan offered him some more, but again the falcon knocked the cup from his hand.

"You may not be thirsty," said the sultan, "but I certainly am." He refilled the cup and went to drink some water. But the falcon flew at his face, knocking the cup once again from his hand.

In a moment of anger, the sultan drew his sword and killed the bird. "No bird may decide when the sultan drinks or doesn't drink!" he said.

Just then he heard a hissing sound coming from the spring. It was a snake in the water, with deadly venom dripping from its jaws.

"Oh no, what have I done?" cried the sultan. He gathered up the falcon in his arms. "The bird was trying to protect me all along. The water I was trying to drink was poisonous."

"So, you see," Yunan said, "this sultan killed the very one who had saved him." He looked at the vizier solemnly. "I'd hate to kill the falcon who saved *me*," he said.

The vizier rubbed his beard. "I agree," he said, "but I'm afraid the doctor is not like the falcon in this story. He is like the serpent. It is me who, like the loyal falcon, is trying to save your life."

The vizier looked so loyal and sincere that the sultan was convinced. "We don't have a moment to lose," he said. "Bring the doctor to me at once."

When the doctor appeared before him, the sultan gave the order: "This man must die immediately, before he murders me."

The doctor gasped. "But I cured you!"

"Only so you could get close enough to kill me," said the sultan. "Off with his head!"

A guard stepped forward and raised his sword.

"Is there nothing I can do to convince you I mean you no harm?" pleaded the doctor.

"Nothing at all," said the sultan.

"If you kill an innocent man, terrible things will happen to you in return," said the doctor. "I ask you again, will you spare me?"

"I will not," said the sultan.

"Then before I die, let me save something valuable that is in my possession," said the doctor. "It is a magical book, the secret powers of which will be lost if I am killed without telling anyone."

The sultan put up his hand to the swordsman. "Wait. What does it do, this book?" he asked.

"It will allow you to keep my knowledge after I am dead," said the doctor, "so if you are ever unwell again, you may be cured."

"Bring me the book!" said the sultan eagerly. The doctor explained to the guards where the book was, and they ran off to find it.

When they returned, the doctor explained. "Once my head is cut off, you must put it on a plate, and read out the instructions from this book," he said. "After that, my head will answer any question asked of it."

"Amazing," said the sultan, opening the book.

"Leaf through the book, and you'll find the instructions," said the doctor.

The pages were stuck together, so the sultan licked his finger to turn the first page. Then he licked it again to turn the second.

Both pages were blank. "There's nothing here," he said, puzzled.

"I think it's a little further on," said the doctor. "Keep going."

The sultan licked his finger and turned the next page, and the next, "I can't see anything," he said. Then suddenly he looked up at the doctor in horror. He gave a strange, strangled cry and collapsed onto the floor.

The pages of the book had been painted with a deadly poison, and the sultan had licked enough from his finger to kill him.

The vizier and the guards rushed to the sultan's side to help him, only to find that the sultan had died on the spot.

"Seize the doctor!" shouted the vizier wildly. The doctor, however, was nowhere to be seen.

So that was the end of Yunan the Magnificent.
As for the doctor, nobody knew where he went,
and he was never, ever seen or heard of again.

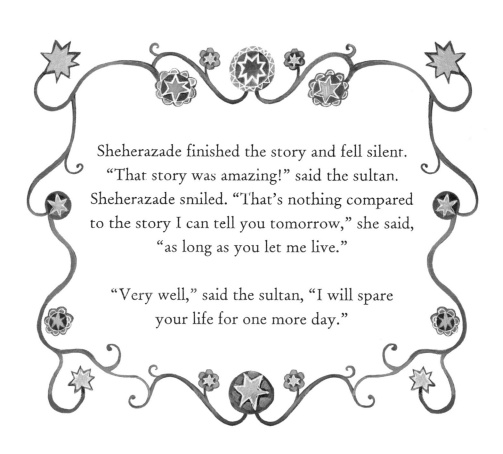

Sheherazade finished the story and fell silent.
"That story was amazing!" said the sultan.
Sheherazade smiled. "That's nothing compared
to the story I can tell you tomorrow," she said,
"as long as you let me live."

"Very well," said the sultan, "I will spare
your life for one more day."

The next night,
when the sultan was settled in his bed,
Sheherazade began…

The Clever Prince, the Princess and the Genie

Once there was a prince who was extremely clever and well-educated. He could solve complicated mathematical problems in his head, he spoke twenty languages and composed heart-rending poetry, which he recorded in the most beautiful handwriting ever seen.

Word spread of his cleverness, and one day the King of India sent a messenger to his father, asking if the prince could come to visit.

The prince's father prepared a ship, and sent his son on a voyage to India. After a month at sea, the ship came to land and the captain lowered the anchor.

"The royal guards will escort you to the palace," he told the prince. The guards started getting ready to go ashore.

"There's really no need," said the prince. "I have studied many maps and I know the way. It's not very far. I will go alone. You may take me ashore and then set sail for home right away."

"Very well," said the captain.

And so he took the prince ashore, along with the many gifts his father had sent for the king.

The prince set off alone, leading a train of camels all laden with the offerings.

He had only gone a mile or so, when a band of robbers attacked him. "Stop," cried the prince. "I've come in peace to see the King of India."

"We don't care who you've come to see," said the robbers. They threw the prince to the ground, stripped off his expensive cloak and gold belt, and then rode away with all the camels, leaving him in the dust with nothing.

He was alone in a foreign land, without as much as a coin in his pocket. "I'll just have to walk there and explain what happened," he thought to himself. So he set off at a brisk pace in the right direction.

It was a wild and barren land, with no towns or villages, no farms or houses to be seen anywhere.

As the prince was trudging along, a sudden whirring noise filled the air, and a bright blue genie swept out of the sky. He flew down to the ground, a little way ahead of the prince, grasped hold of a huge rock and rolled it aside to reveal a hole in the ground. Then the genie disappeared into the hole.

The prince didn't think the genie had noticed him, so he crept quietly to the opening and listened. "Please let me go," he heard a woman's sweet voice say. "I can never love you, not even if you keep me here forever."

"You will learn to," said a deep, booming voice, which the prince took to be the genie's. "You are mine, and I will keep you here for as long as I like. I will return in two days and see whether you love me then."

The prince ducked out of sight as the genie came whirling up out of the cave. He rolled the rock back across the entrance, then whooshed up into the sky and was gone.

"I must save whoever is trapped down there," thought the prince. He pushed and shoved at the rock, but he wasn't strong enough to move it. So he searched the ground for some sturdy branches, and brought them back. Then he wedged them beneath the edge of the rock and used them to lever up the rock. He pushed with all his might, and the rock rolled aside.

The prince crept down into the gloom. A dark passageway was lit at the end with glimmering candlelight. "Hello," he called as he drew near to the light. "Don't be afraid. I've come to save you."

He turned the corner into a large underground cavern, to find the most beautiful girl he had ever seen standing there with eyes as wide as a deer's. "Who are you?" she asked.

"I'm a prince. I was on my way to visit the King of India when I was attacked by robbers," the prince explained. "I happened to be walking this way, and I saw the genie. So I decided to help you if I could."

"Thank you," said the princess, gratefully.

"That is a very happy coincidence. The King of India is my father. I was kidnapped by the genie shortly after my father wrote to you."

"He must be sick with worry," said the prince. He glanced around the cave, which was luxuriously furnished and had walls lined with hundreds of books. There was an ornate dining table with bowls of luscious fruit on it, and a bed covered in embroidered cushions. The whole cavern was lit with glowing candles.

"The genie wants me to be his wife, and to consider this my home," said the princess, following the prince's gaze with her own. "It's comfortable. But it's a prison, nonetheless."

"Then escape with me now," urged the prince.

The princess smiled. "I will," she said. "But first let us eat. The genie won't return for two days, so we may as well prepare ourselves for the journey ahead."

They sat down at the table and ate and talked about many things. The princess told the prince that many of the genie's books were about magic. She had been studying them since she had been imprisoned. None of the magic she had learned seemed to work in the cave, though. "It may be because of some other spell the genie has cast on this place, to keep me here," she said. "Or perhaps I don't know enough magic yet to defeat him."

They talked until it was late, and the prince began to feel more and more admiration for the princess. This feeling welled up and up inside him and in the end he could contain himself no longer. He stood up, slammed his fist down on the table and shouted, "I wish the genie would come back now. Then I could kill him and you could marry me instead."

To his surprise, the princess went pale with horror. "You have summoned the genie," she cried. "He will be here in an instant. Quick! Run!" And the princess immediately fled the cavern out into the dark night.

The prince was so surprised he stood there for a moment too long. There was a whirring noise outside the cave and, before he knew it, the blue genie was standing there before him.

"Where is she?" the genie thundered, his face purple with rage. "What have you done with her?" He grabbed the prince around his middle, and swept out of the cave into the night.

The prince found himself dangling in the

sky from the genie's colossal fist, as the
scanned the ground below for the princess.
ere IS she?" demanded the genie, shaking the
ce until he thought his bones would break.

I hope the princess is long gone by now,"
said the prince. "Do with me as you will."

In the end, the genie flew back to the ground
and threw down the prince in fury. "I'll teach you
to meddle in my affairs," he roared.

In a flash, the genie turned the prince into
a monkey with a long, curly tail. Despite
understanding twenty languages, now the prince
could only make monkey noises instead of
speaking a word that anyone could understand.

He bounded off into the night, leaving the
genie pounding deep chasms into the ground
with rage and frustration.

Three days later, a monkey appeared at the King of India's palace. It leaped in through the window and chattered nonsensically at the king. The king, who was in high spirits because his beloved daughter had returned home, chuckled at the creature. "Look darling," he said to the princess. "This monkey has something it wants to tell us."

The princess smiled sadly. "I'm sorry, Father," she said. "I can't bring myself to laugh at the antics of a monkey, when I'm not sure whether the prince who saved me is dead or alive." The monkey turned somersaults at that, and chattered even more loudly.

The king looked at his daughter fondly. "I'm so grateful to him, whoever he is. My soldiers are doing all they can to find him, my dear.

Let's take your mind off it. Do you want to continue our game of chess?"

The princess shook her head. "I should get back to studying," she said. Since returning home, she had been learning all about magical ways to defeat a genie. Her father swore that his army would keep her safe, but the princess really wanted to be prepared to defend herself.

Her father watched her go and shook his head. "I don't suppose you can finish the game with me?" he joked to the monkey.

To his amusement, the monkey nodded its head, and settled down opposite him. It rubbed its chin for a moment, and then, quite deliberately, moved the queen all the way across the board.

"Well I never," exclaimed the King of India,

examining the pieces. "It's checkmate. You've won the game." He stared in astonishment at the monkey before him. "You are a clever little fellow. What else can you do?"

Just then, the king's advisor came in bearing a scroll for the king to sign. "Do you want me to get rid of that creature for you?" he asked, looking down his nose at the monkey.

"No, no," said the king, taking the scroll and quill pen. In a split second, the monkey snatched them from him and climbed up a pillar. It perched on a carved stone lotus flower near the ceiling and started scribbling frantically.

"Come back with that, you stupid creature," shouted the advisor.

But the king, who was staring closely at the monkey, said, "Wait a minute. I do believe it's writing something."

After a few minutes, the monkey came back down the pillar and handed the scroll to the king. It was covered in the most delicate, elegant writing. The king began to read. The writing described, in perfect verse, how the monkey had once been a clever prince, but that he had been turned into a monkey after trying to save the Princess of India.

"Extraordinary," said the king. To his advisor, he said, "Call my daughter, please."

When his daughter came, the monkey bowed low before her, and the king handed her the scroll to read. She finished it with tears in her eyes. Then she knelt and took the monkey's hand.

"Is it really you?" she asked. Then she said, "Wait… I know how to tell. If it is you, tell me what it was that summoned the genie back."

At once, the monkey ran over to the table and slammed its fist down on it.

"Yes," cried the princess. "That was it."

A terrible, deafening voice echoed through the room. "And it has summoned me again. Now I can take you back, my darling."

To everybody's horror, the blue genie whirled into the room through the open window. His bulk towered above the princess, her father, and the monkey. The advisor whimpered and crawled under the table to hide.

"Guards, seize him!" cried the king. But no one came.

The genie let out a nasty, booming laugh.

"I have put all your guards to sleep," he said.

"Run, my dear!" the king urged the princess.

But the princess stood her ground. "I'm not going anywhere," she said. She folded her arms and glared up at the genie. "I'm ready to fight you now," she declared.

The genie laughed even louder, making the palace walls tremble.

Then suddenly he turned into a large, ferocious lion and leaped at the princess with his teeth bared.

The princess plucked a hair from her head and muttered a spell. In a twinkling of an eye, the hair became a sword, and she cut the lion in two.

The two halves joined
together again. They
became a giant scorpion,
which ran at the princess,
raising its tail to strike.

The princess turned
into a serpent and slithered
quickly out of the scorpion's way.

The scorpion transformed into
an eagle and dived at the serpent
ready to seize it in its claws.

The serpent became a vulture
and swooped up out of the way.

It turned on the eagle, which
sped out of the window, with
the vulture in hot pursuit.

The monkey and the king
ran to the window to watch.

The vulture pursued the
eagle and drove it down to the
courtyard. The eagle landed, and
the vulture was about to seize it
when it became a black cat. It turned
and hissed, swiping its claws at the vulture.

In a flash, the vulture became a silver wolf.
It snarled ferociously at the cat and pounced.

The two fought fiercely, but just as the wolf cornered the cat, it turned into a red pomegranate and rolled away. The wolf leaped on it, and split it in half, and the seeds scattered all the way across the courtyard.

The wolf turned into a hen, which began pecking up the seeds as fast as it could. The very last seed was trapped between the cobblestones. The hen pecked and pecked at it, but she couldn't reach it.

Then the seed turned into a fish, which flip-flopped across the courtyard and plunged into the fountain.

The hen scurried after it. As she leaped into the fountain, she turned into a giant whale. The creature crashed through the fountain, shattering the marble to pieces and spilling the water all across the courtyard.

The blue genie squeezed himself out from beneath the whale's belly. He had fire in his eyes and smoke coming from his nostrils.

"Now I'm angry," he bellowed. "Now I'm really angry."

The whale was suddenly a princess again, who yelled, "You're not the only one!"

"That's my girl!" shouted the king from the window, and the genie glared up at him.

"What are you looking at?" the genie roared, and lunged towards him. But the princess leaped in his way, and flung up her hands. A stream of flames came from her palms and engulfed the genie. "In the name of God and all things good, I defeat you. You are no more!" she cried.

And, to everyone's astonishment and relief, the genie was turned into a pile of ashes.

The princess pressed her palms together and smiled. "That's the end of HIM," she said with some satisfaction. Then she looked up at the window where her father and the monkey stood. "Monkey, my dear, please bring me some water," she called. The monkey seized a cup from the table and clambered quickly down the wall to join her in the courtyard.

She took the cup from him, dipped her fingers into the water and sprinkled it on the monkey's head. "In the name of God and all things good," she said, "be yourself and a monkey no more!"

The monkey became the prince again and took her in his arms. "I've never met anyone as clever or as brave as you," he said.

The princess smiled. "I like you much better as a man than as a monkey," she said.

"Do you like me well enough to marry me?" asked the prince.

To which the princess said, "I do."

They were married the very next day, much to the delight of the princess's father. And when the prince brought his wife home from India, everybody was astonished by the wonderful stories they had to tell.

Sheherazade finished the story and fell silent. "That story was amazing!" said the sultan. Sheherazade smiled. "That's nothing compared to the story I can tell you tomorrow," she said, "as long as you let me live."

"Very well," said the sultan, "I will spare your life for one more day."

The next night,
when the sultan was settled in his bed,
Sheherazade began...

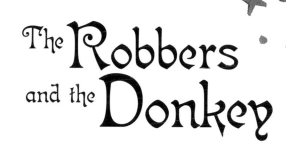

The Robbers and the Donkey

A man was leading his donkey along the road when two robbers crept up behind him. One robber slipped the rope from around the donkey's neck and put it around his own neck. The other quietly led the donkey away.

The owner didn't notice a thing. As far as he was concerned, he was still leading his donkey along until all of a sudden it stopped and would go no further. It was then that he turned around. He was flabbergasted to see that where his donkey had been there was now a man standing with a rope around his neck.

"Who on Earth are you?" he asked.

"I'm your donkey," replied the robber. "That is to say, I *was* your donkey. It's a very strange story..."

"I'm all ears," said the man.

"Well, I used to be a man," the robber began. "But one day I did something naughty, and everything changed. You see, I was horribly rude to my mother. She slaved over a hot stove all day to cook a wonderful meal for me. I came home really late, and the food was spoiled. But I didn't apologize. In fact, when my mother grumbled about my bad manners, I pushed her out of the house and slammed the door in her face."

"That's no way for a son to treat his mother," scolded the man.

"No," agreed the robber, "but what happened next is worse than that."

"Go on," the man urged.

"She chanted a spell outside my door, knocked three times, then shouted, 'Onky, plonky, turn into a donkey!'" the robber continued. "My ears grew long and my teeth stuck out, my face changed shape and I fell on all fours. Before I knew it, I had turned into a donkey. My mother opened the door and drove me out of the house. She chased me all around the town with a broom until I ran away, and I haven't seen her since."

"That's no way for a mother to treat her son!" exclaimed the man.

"Exactly," said the robber.

"Tell me," said the man. "How did you end up in the market where I bought you?"

"A merchant found me on the street and took me there to make some money," said the robber. "I was so lucky it was you who bought me," he added, smiling winningly at the man. "You've been so kind to me all the time I was your donkey, and that must have broken the spell. I'm eternally grateful to you."

The man untied the rope from around the robber's neck, "No problem," he said. "Good luck to you, and goodbye."

The robber shook his hand solemnly, biting his lip so he wouldn't laugh, and ran off to find his friend.

The man went home, his head spinning at how strange the world was. When he told his wife what had happened, she said, "That's awful if it's true. But what will we do without a donkey? We need it to pull the cart. You had better go to market and buy another one."

Later that day, the man was browsing around the market place, looking at all the donkeys for sale. Imagine his surprise when he came across his very own donkey. "It can't be true," he thought.

He looked the donkey over from head to tail. It had a tooth missing, just like his old donkey. It had a little tuft of white hairs in its tail, just like his old donkey. It had a little nick in its left front

hoof, just like his old donkey. This was, beyond a shadow of a doubt, his old donkey.

The man frowned at the donkey and whispered in its hairy ear. "You naughty rascal. Have you been rude to your mother again? I'm not saving you a second time!"

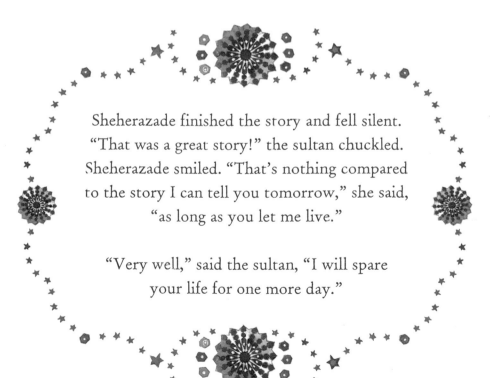

Sheherazade finished the story and fell silent. "That was a great story!" the sultan chuckled. Sheherazade smiled. "That's nothing compared to the story I can tell you tomorrow," she said, "as long as you let me live."

"Very well," said the sultan, "I will spare your life for one more day."

The next night,
when the sultan was settled in his bed,
Sheherazade began...

Aladdin
and the
Magic Lamp

laddin was hanging around doing nothing, as usual, when a stranger approached him in the street. It was a man wearing embroidered robes. He had a long beard and a strange, piercing look in his eye. "Are you Aladdin, the tailor's son?" he asked.

Aladdin nodded, surprised that the stranger knew him. He was even more taken aback when the man let out a loud wail and flung his arms around him. "It's really you!" the stranger cried.

"What are you talking about?" Aladdin asked, pulling himself free. "Who are you?"

The man looked shocked. "Did your father, my brother, never mention me?" he whispered.

"No. My father died years ago," Aladdin said. "It's just my mother and me now."

The stranger sobbed dramatically into his sleeve. "That's why I'm here." he sniffed. "I finally learned of my brother's death and I've come back to take care of you, my dear nephew."

He pressed a gold coin into Aladdin's palm, and said, "Give this to your mother. Tell her your uncle is coming for dinner, and to prepare a feast.

There's plenty more where that came from."

Aladdin nodded. "We live in the old tailor's shop at the end of this street. See you later, Uncle," he said, and ran off home. The stranger watched him go with a cold smile on his face.

Little did Aladdin know, but the man was an evil sorcerer. He'd read a book of magic that said that something of great power was held in an enchanted underground garden in this city. But the only person who could take it without being turned to stone was a poor boy named Aladdin.

"My rich uncle's coming to dinner!" Aladdin sang as his mother opened the front door.

"Don't talk nonsense, Aladdin," his mother scolded. "You don't have any uncles."

"He gave me this," said Aladdin, handing her the coin, "and said to make a feast for tonight."

His mother's eyes grew round at the sight of money. She bustled off to the market at once. By the time there was a knock on the front door, she had prepared a wonderful meal.

Aladdin opened the door, and in came the sorcerer with heaps of gifts. He had cakes, wine, and a flagon of perfume for Aladdin's mother.

After putting everything down, the sorcerer bowed low before Aladdin's mother. "Dear sister, I am so pleased to meet you at last," he said in a sugar-sweet voice.

"I-I'm so sorry we've never met before," stammered Aladdin's mother, overwhelmed.

The man fell at her feet, sobbing, "My poor brother. I wish I'd seen him again before he died."

"There, there," cooed Aladdin's mother. "You're here now, and that's what matters."

"Yes," the sorcerer beamed. "I have vowed to take care of you, and that's just what I'll do." They sat down to eat, and he asked Aladdin, "So, my boy, what trade are you learning?"

Aladdin blushed and lowered his head.

"Aladdin refuses to learn anything," his mother said. "I despair of him."

"That won't do," said the sorcerer. "Name any job you wish to have, Aladdin, and I'll see to it."

The boy squirmed in his seat. He didn't want to have to work, but he didn't dare say so.

The sorcerer saw exactly what the matter was. "How about I open a shop for you and fill it with perfumes? You could just sit there and the money would pour in," he suggested with a sly smile.

Aladdin couldn't believe his ears. "Yes, please, Uncle," he beamed.

The next day the sorcerer took Aladdin to the finest suit shop in town. Aladdin emerged dressed in turquoise silk and grinning from ear to ear. They went to a fancy restaurant for lunch, and then strolled around to choose the best street for Aladdin's shop.

The following morning, the sorcerer said to Aladdin, "We'll open your shop tomorrow. First, there's something I want to show you. Come with me." He set off at a brisk pace, and Aladdin had to run to keep up.

The sorcerer took Aladdin to the royal parks, where he marched around until he found a small archway. He led Aladdin through it into a hidden part of the park. A broad smile spread across his face. "Here it is!" he exclaimed, clapping the bewildered boy on the back.

The sorcerer gathered some sticks and lit a fire. Then he reached inside his robes and brought out a tiny box. Muttering a charm, he took a pinch of powder from the box and cast it into the flames.

With a BOOM, a huge puff of purple smoke rose from the fire, and the earth split open to reveal a stone door in the ground.

It was too much for Aladdin. He turned to run away, but was seized by the scruff of the neck. "Where do you think you're going?" snarled the sorcerer, the mask of kindness slipping from his face.

Seeing the shocked look on Aladdin's face, the sorcerer quickly recovered his smile.

"Aladdin, trust me. I'm your uncle." he wheedled. "If you do as I say, you'll go home a rich man."

Aladdin gulped. "What must I do?" he asked.

"First, open the door," said the sorcerer.

Aladdin took hold of the door knob and heaved. To his surprise, the door opened easily to reveal a deep hole. "Just as it said in the book," the sorcerer muttered, smiling to himself.

"Now pay attention," he continued. "Down there you'll find an oil lamp and lots of treasure. As long as you bring me the lamp, you may help yourself to as much treasure as you like." Then he took a ring from his finger and put it on the boy's. "This ring will protect you," he said. Then he lowered Aladdin down into the hole.

At the bottom there was a corridor that led further underground. Aladdin crept along it and found himself in the most wonderful garden full of trees bearing all kinds of sparkling jewels.

He wandered around until he found a battered, dull brass lamp hanging from a hook on the wall. "That doesn't look like anything special," he thought. But he tucked it in his shirt and rushed back to the trees.

After picking as many jewels as he could carry, Aladdin returned to the sorcerer. "Pull me up," he said, too heavily laden to climb out by himself.

"Pass me the lamp first," said the sorcerer.

"I can't. I've got piles of jewels on top of it in my shirt," said Aladdin. "Just give me your hand."

The sorcerer's eyes narrowed. "Don't try to trick me, boy. Give me the lamp!"

"You can have it as soon as I'm out," said Aladdin.

But the sorcerer assumed Aladdin was trying to keep the lamp for himself. He flew into a rage. "If I can't have it, nobody can!" he cried, and he slammed the heavy stone door shut.

Aladdin heard him murmur a charm to seal the rock. "Don't leave me here!" he wailed.

But there was no reply. It suddenly dawned on Aladdin that he had been fooled. "That man wasn't my uncle," he sobbed. "He only wanted me to get this stupid lamp. I'm going to die here!"

As he wrung his hands in desperation, Aladdin accidentally rubbed the ring the sorcerer had given him. In a flash of light, a purple genie appeared. "How may I serve you, Master?" the genie asked.

Aladdin's hair stood on end. He'd never seen a genie before. "Who– what– are you?" he stammered, his voice hoarse with fear.

"I am the genie of the ring," said the genie. "Since you are wearing the ring, you may command me to do anything."

"Can you get me out of here?" Aladdin asked.

"Your wish is my command," said the genie.

In a puff of smoke, Aladdin found himself standing alone outside his house. He rushed inside and told his mother what had happened.

"I should never have trusted that man," she moaned. "At least you're safe now."

"Not only that," said Aladdin, "but I have some things to sell at the market." He poured the gems out on the table and put down the oil lamp.

Aladdin's mother was speechless for a moment. Then she frowned at the grubby lamp. "You could sell that too, if it was a bit cleaner," she said. She picked it up and gave it a good rub.

There was a puff of smoke, and an enormous blue genie appeared. "How may I serve you?" he boomed. Aladdin's mother took one look and keeled over in a dead faint.

Aladdin, who was more used to genies by now, said, "Bring us something to eat, please."

"Your wish is my command," said the genie. In the twinkling of an eye, he vanished and reappeared carrying several gold dishes piled with a feast fit for a king. He laid them on the table and disappeared again.

Aladdin fanned his mother's face.

"Has he gone?" she asked when she came to.

"Never mind about that," said Aladdin. "Let's sit down and eat."

They'd never tasted such fine food. When they had finished, Aladdin examined the plates. "These must be worth a penny or two," he said.

"Are they ours to sell?" asked his mother. "Wasn't that a genie? I don't think we should meddle with him. Let's get rid of the lamp."

"No way!" said Aladdin. "With that lamp, we can get whatever we want, whenever we want it."

That afternoon, Aladdin took the plates to the market to sell, and came home a good deal richer. When his mother saw the money he'd made, she decided he could keep the lamp after all.

For a few weeks they lived contentedly. Each evening the genie provided a fine meal, and each morning Aladdin would sell the plates it had been served on. He and his mother could afford to buy everything they wanted and more.

One day, when Aladdin went to the market, there was a tremendous crowd. "Make way!" came a shout, and a royal procession appeared. Everyone in the marketplace bowed their heads low, but Aladdin stood and stared.

A fruit seller hissed at him, "Lower your head before it's chopped off! The princess is coming."

Aladdin ducked his head, but as the carriage passed by, he stole a glance at the princess. When he saw her, Aladdin felt dizzy with delight. She was more beautiful than he ever could have imagined. The boy stumbled home in a haze of happiness.

"What on earth is the matter with you?" asked his mother.

"I'm in love," sighed Aladdin dreamily.

"With whom?" his mother asked.

"The emperor's daughter," Aladdin replied.

His mother grew pale. "They kill men just for looking at the princess," she said.

"I'm going to marry her," said Aladdin.

His mother's mouth dropped open. "Are you crazy?" she whispered.

"No," said Aladdin. Snapping into action, he gathered all the gems together in a gold bowl. "Please can you take this as a present to the emperor, and ask for the princess's hand in marriage for me?" he asked.

His mother sat down at the table. "How can I ask the emperor whether his only daughter will marry the son of a tailor?" she asked.

But Aladdin wouldn't take no for an answer,

so his mother went to see the emperor. She threw herself to her knees before him and said, "Before I ask what I'm about to ask, I need to beg forgiveness for asking it."

The emperor tried to hide a smile. "Don't worry," he said. "I won't be angry."

"Very well then," said Aladdin's mother. "I'm here to ask for your daughter's hand in marriage on behalf of my son."

"What impertinence!" shouted the emperor. A murmur of agreement went around the hall.

Then Aladdin's mother uncovered the bowl of jewels. "He said to give you this," she added.

The murmur turned to a gasp as the jewels lit up the whole room. The emperor stared in amazement. "I have never seen such large jewels," he admitted.

Just then, the emperor's advisor cleared his throat loudly. The emperor had promised him that the princess could marry his son, and the advisor didn't want his majesty to forget that promise.

The emperor glanced at him. To Aladdin's mother he said, "Thank you for your gift. Come back in a month, and I'll reconsider your request."

Aladdin's mother hurried home and told her son. "That means yes!" he crowed. He grabbed his mother and danced her around the room.

Nothing wiped the smile off Aladdin's face for a whole week. But one day, on his way to the market, he notice the streets were decorated with flags. "What's going on?" he asked a girl.

"Have you had your head in the ground?" she mocked. "The princess married the son of the emperor's advisor this morning!"

Aladdin stared at her. "But she's promised to me!" he protested. He ran home with a chorus of laughter at his back.

All day long, Aladdin strode back and forth wondering what to do. In the evening, when his mother had gone to bed, he rubbed the lamp. "I want you to bring the princess to me," Aladdin said to the genie, "and to put her husband on top of a snowy mountain."

"Your wish is my command," the genie replied.

Moments later, a very bewildered princess appeared. "Am I dreaming?" she asked.

"Don't be afraid," Aladdin said gently. "Sit down with me and let's talk for a while."

The princess sat down nervously, and Aladdin talked to her. He told her stories of his childhood. Before long, the princess forgot how strange the situation was. She began to laugh and tell stories of her own. When the two grew tired, they lay down side by side and fell asleep.

Early the next morning, while the princess slept, Aladdin summoned the genie. "Please take the princess and her husband home," he said.

"Your wish is my command, Aladdin," replied the genie.

The sleeping princess was whisked away. When she awoke to find herself in her own bed with a half-frozen, speechless husband next to her, she didn't know what to think.

That night, Aladdin ordered the genie once more to bring him the princess, and put her husband on top of a mountain.

This time when the princess arrived, she gave a slight smile. "You again," she said. "I don't know what this is all about...but since I'm here, you might as well tell me some more stories."

Again, they talked and talked late into the night. When the princess finally fell asleep Aladdin gazed at her long black hair tumbling over her shoulders. "She's so beautiful," he thought. "I hope this plan works."

When the princess and her chilly husband were returned to their bedroom on the second morning, neither could find anything to say to the other.

On the third night, when the princess appeared in Aladdin's house, she beamed at him with delight. "You're so much more fun than my cold, dreary husband," she said. "I wish I could spend my days with you instead of just dreaming about it."

The next morning at breakfast, the emperor noticed the princess and her new husband looking glum. "Is there something wrong?" he asked them.

The advisor's son burst out, "I can't take any more! I don't want to spend every night for the rest of my life on top of a snowy mountain. I want out of this marriage. Now!"

The baffled emperor looked at his daughter, who nodded her agreement. "Very well, then," he sighed. And so the marriage was declared over.

The next day, Aladdin's mother paid the emperor another visit. She stepped up to the throne nervously and bowed before him.

"You told me to come back in a month," she said. "So here I am. Please, your highness, may my son marry your daughter?"

The emperor looked at her wearily. His daughter's marriage may have failed, but there was no way he was giving her up to just anyone. "If your son can bring me forty dishes filled with gold, carried by forty dancing women," he said, "then he may propose to my daughter."

Aladdin's mother bustled off home. Ten minutes later, there was a tremendous noise outside, and the emperor's advisor rushed into the throne room, pale and shaking.

"What's the matter?" asked the emperor.

"You'd better see for yourself," was the reply.

When the emperor went outside, he couldn't believe his eyes.

Trumpets sounded, cymbals crashed, pipes blew. Approaching the palace were forty dancing women carrying forty dishes, each filled with glowing gold. Behind them marched forty elephants, carrying forty musicians on their backs. In the middle, riding on a white horse, was Aladdin, looking for all the world like a prince. He was scattering gold coins to the townspeople, who cheered and cheered.

The emperor came to greet him. Aladdin got down from his horse and bowed. "Your Majesty, I've come to propose to your daughter," he said.

The emperor could do nothing but nod. He waved his hand and his daughter was brought out. When she saw Aladdin she couldn't stop smiling.

"Will you marry me?" asked Aladdin.

"I will," the princess replied happily.

Aladdin and the princess were married the very next day. Over the wedding feast, the emperor confided in Aladdin. "My daughter is precious to me. I want you to promise to look after her. Also, I want you to live near my palace."

"I understand," said Aladdin.

The next morning when the emperor looked out of his bedroom window he nearly fell over in astonishment. There, in front of his palace, stood another palace. It had appeared from nowhere. And what a grand palace it was. It had pink walls and hundreds of pretty domes and spires.

He went outside to find Aladdin and the princess admiring it. "Isn't it amazing?" said the princess. And the emperor had to agree.

A few weeks later, when Aladdin was out helping his mother move into a new house, the princess heard a voice outside calling. "New lamps for old! New lamps for old!"

"How strange," she thought. But, remembering a battered old lamp Aladdin had brought with him when they got married, she thought it might be fun to surprise him with a new one.

So she rushed outside with the lamp, and found a strange man with piercing eyes. "New lamps for old," he called.

"I have one," the princess said, and she gave him the battered old lamp.

The man's eyes lit up as he examined the lamp. He thrust a shiny new lamp into the princess's hands, and hurried away.

When Aladdin returned home, the princess and their entire palace had vanished. The emperor was outside with tears rolling down his face, "Where is my daughter?" he sobbed.

"I don't know," said Aladdin miserably. "But I'll bring her back, I promise." Then he thought to himself, "I bet the sorcerer is at the bottom of this," and he set off that minute to find him.

Aladdin rode through cities, towns and villages, through snowy mountains and scorching deserts. Then, just as he was getting desperate, he remembered that he was still wearing the sorcerer's magic ring. He rubbed it, and the purple genie appeared. "How may I serve you, Master?" he asked.

"Please bring the princess and our palace back at once," Aladdin ordered.

The purple genie shook his head. "I am not powerful enough to undo what a blue genie has done," he said. "But I can take you to your wife."

"That's good enough," said Aladdin.

In a puff of purple smoke, he found himself standing in a hot, dry land, right next to the pink palace. He heard the princess's voice coming from the window. "I wish Aladdin were here."

He scaled the wall and climbed in through the window. When the princess saw him, she nearly fainted with delight. "An evil old man stole me away," she told Aladdin. "He asked me to be his wife. When I refused, he locked me in here and told me I couldn't resist his charms forever. Aladdin, what can we do? He must be really powerful. He whisked the palace across the world, and he has a blue genie who does whatever he tells him."

Aladdin smiled wryly. "That blue genie lives in the old lamp I used to have."

The princess gasped. "I'm so sorry," she said. "I gave the lamp to the old man."

"You couldn't have known," said Aladdin. "But now we need to come up with a plan..."

When the sorcerer came to visit the princess the following morning, he found her dressed in her prettiest outfit, smiling at him. "Have you changed your mind?" he asked in surprise.

"Perhaps," said the princess. "I wondered if we could get to know one another over lunch?"

The sorcerer grinned horribly and rubbed his hands together. The princess shivered in disgust.

"I'll pick you up later," the sorcerer said.

When he had left, Aladdin appeared at the window and handed the princess a tiny bottle.

"The genie of the ring brought me this sleeping potion," he said. "All you need to do is slip it into the sorcerer's drink somehow."

That afternoon, the sorcerer escorted the princess to lunch. "You're as beautiful as the glitter of diamonds," he crooned.

"You're about as handsome as a toad," thought the princess. But she smiled and said, "How can I resist such powerful charms?"

She sat down and the sorcerer kissed her hand. "You're as sweet as syrup," he gloated.

The princess felt quite unwell. But she said as sweetly as she could, "There's a custom in my land for lovers to drink from one another's cups." Smiling innocently at the sorcerer, she slid her goblet behind a large pile of grapes and poured the sleeping potion into the wine.

The sorcerer sidled up to her. The princess raised her cup to his lips, and he put his cup to hers. "After this you'll be all mine?" he leered.

"Let's drink to that," the princess whispered, and took a sip of the sorcerer's wine.

No sooner had he gulped down her wine, than the sleeping potion took effect. He keeled over onto his back and started snoring loudly.

"Thank goodness for that," sighed the princess. "Aladdin," she called. "You can come in now."

Aladdin entered the room and picked up the lamp. Summoning the genie, he said, "Please take us home. We'll drop the sorcerer off on the way..."

That evening, the sorcerer awoke stranded on

top of a mountain, while Aladdin and the princess were being welcomed home by her father.

After that, Aladdin and the princess were so happy they never wished for anything else. The lamp and the magic ring lay forgotten in a drawer somewhere... Who knows, perhaps they have genies in them still.

Sheherazade finished the story and fell silent. "That story was amazing!" said the sultan. Sheherazade smiled. "That's nothing compared to the story I can tell you tomorrow," she said, "as long as you let me live."

"Very well," said the sultan, "I will spare your life for one more day."

The next night,
when the sultan was settled in his bed,
Sheherazade began...

The Flying Horse

There once was a king who had two daughters as pretty as wild flowers, and a son as handsome as the moon. Their beauty and goodness were famed far and wide, and everybody in the kingdom dreamed of marrying one of them.

One day, three sorcerers came to the palace with gifts for the king. Two were young and handsome, and one was older and very ugly.

The first sorcerer brought a magnificent clockwork peacock that marked each passing hour. It spread its gold and sapphire tail feathers, opened its gold beak and sang out the time. The king was delighted.

"How can I reward you?" he asked. "Would you like a coffer of gold?"

The first sorcerer shook his head. "There's nothing I'd like more," he said, "than to ask your elder daughter to marry me."

"If she wants to marry you, I've nothing against the match," said the king, and he called for his elder daughter to meet the sorcerer.

The second sorcerer brought a golden trumpet which, when hung over the city gates, blasted loudly whenever an enemy passed through the gate.

"How can I thank you?" asked the king. "Would you like a coffer of gold?"

The sorcerer shook his head. "There's nothing I'd like more," he said, "than to ask your younger daughter to marry me."

"If she wants to marry you, I've nothing against the match," said the king, and he called for his younger daughter to meet the sorcerer.

The third brought a beautifully carved ebony horse that could take the rider anywhere in the world. He presented it grumpily, knowing there were no daughters left for him to marry.

"I'm sure my son would really like to see this," said the king, and he called for the prince.

The prince was very interested in the ebony horse. "How does it work?" he asked.

"By magic," said the sorcerer sulkily. "You sit on it and it takes you where you wish to go."

The prince climbed on the horse's back, eager to try it out. "What do I do?" he asked, fiddling with the reins. The sorcerer was just about to reply, when the prince discovered a tiny lever on the horse's right shoulder. He pulled the lever, and the horse rose straight up into the sky.

The prince gazed beneath him at his father's kingdom, which reached all the way to the sea. "I wish I could see how far the sea stretches," he thought, and before he knew it the horse was sweeping him off in the direction of the sea.

Back down on the ground, the princesses declared themselves happy with their young sorcerers, and the king was busy granting his permission for them to get married.

"What about me?" the third sorcerer asked him crossly. "What do I get?"

The king turned back to answer him, only to find his son and the ebony horse gone. "Where's my son?" he asked.

"He took off with the horse," was the sorcerer's sullen reply.

The king stared in alarm at the empty sky. "Well bring him back!" he ordered.

"I can't. You have to sit on the horse to steer it," said the sorcerer. "Your son took off before I could tell him how it worked. Anyway, what's my reward? My present was by far the best."

The king glared at him. "Your reward for losing my son?" he asked, barely containing his anger. "You shall be flung in the dungeon until he is returned to me." And the guards dragged the sorcerer away.

Up in the air, the prince was having the time of his life. He'd found that while the lever on the right made the horse rise, the lever on the left made it descend. Other than that, he only had to wish to go somewhere for it to fly that way.

So far, he had flown all around his father's kingdom, and now he wanted some adventure. "If only this horse could take me to find the perfect princess for me," he wished. "But I don't know where she would be..."

Before he knew it, the horse was sweeping the prince away, over the sparkling sea to a foreign land, over vast golden deserts, and snowcapped purple mountains. Night fell and the stars came out and twinkled all around him, and still the horse flew on.

Eventually, it came to a sleeping city, with pretty domes and tall spires all silvery in the moonlight, and hovered over a grand palace. The prince pushed the left lever and landed the horse gently on the roof.

Unbeknown to the prince, this palace belonged to a princess who was said to be more beautiful than the moon. To the princess, however, her beauty was a burden and the palace felt like a prison. Her father didn't think any man was good enough for her, and sent away suitor after suitor.

As luck would have it, the princess was taking a moonlit walk in the garden when the prince came sliding down the wall from the roof. They came face to face with one another and were both speechless with surprise and delight.

"Are you the Indian prince who asked my father if he could marry me?" asked the princess. "You are far more handsome than he said you were."

"I'm not him," chuckled the prince. "I've come from afar seeking my true love, and I believe you are the one."

The princess's face shone with the most beautiful smile. They walked and talked for hours, and before they knew it they were deeply in love. "My father refuses to allow anyone to marry me," the princess said sadly. "This time will be no different, no matter how much I love you."

"I'll have to make sure he can't refuse me," said the prince.

They spent all night talking, and all the next day, until the rosy sun was beginning to set. Suddenly the princess's father burst through the garden gates. "Good evening, my dearest—" he began. But when he saw the prince there, he spluttered and turned purple with rage. "Who are you?" he demanded.

"I am a prince seeking my true love," said the prince. "And I am happy to have found her."

"I will call my army and have them tear you to pieces for even suggesting such a thing!" roared the king, and the princess turned pale.

"That's no way to speak to an honest man," the prince said mildly. "I realize this isn't the best way to ask for your daughter's hand in marriage, but I think you will see I am a good match for her, if you only calm down."

"I will not calm down," raged the king. "I'm calling my army!"

"Very well, if you insist. But I will defeat your entire army tomorrow morning on the battlefield," said the prince.

The princess turned even paler, and the king said, "You certainly think a lot of yourself, young man. You'll never defeat an army alone. But it's agreed. Tomorrow you can fight my entire army."

Despite his anger, the king was curious about the prince, so he insisted that he come to stay at his palace. They ate dinner together, and by the time they said goodnight, the king found himself wishing he hadn't ordered the army to fight the boy. He had grown very fond of him.

When morning broke, the princess climbed to the highest tower to watch the battle. The king's army lined up on one side of the battlefield, and the prince walked to the other side alone.

The king joined him. "Are you sure you

won't change your mind about this foolish battle?" he asked uncomfortably.

"Not at all," said the prince breezily. "The only thing is, I can't be expected to fight without my horse. Could you send someone to get it?"

"By all means," said the king. "Where is it?" The prince told him where the horse would be found, and four soldiers went to bring it down from the roof.

The soldiers were smothering smiles as they carried the ebony horse onto the battlefield. "You're not going to get far on this thing!" giggled one of the soldiers.

The king looked concerned. But the prince mounted his horse. "What are we waiting for?" he demanded. So, reluctantly, the king gave the order for the battle to begin.

The army advanced on the prince from across the field, while he sat on his horse and waited. As the soldiers got nearer, they surrounded the horse. They hesitated for a moment or two. Then the captain muttered, "Um– well– CHARGE!" and they all rushed at the prince.

To the soldiers' great astonishment, the horse rose directly up into the air, and they all ran in to one another. Untangling themselves and their weapons, they turned to find the prince had landed in the middle of the battlefield. "Come on then," he laughed.

They charged again. This time, the first line of soldiers leaped at the prince, but he took off so quickly that they missed and fell on their faces. The soldiers behind tripped over them and they all landed in a heap. It was absolute chaos.

The so-called battle went on like this until the king was holding his sides laughing, the princess was giggling and the soldiers were red-faced and exhausted. "We can't fight like this," panted the captain. "It's not a fair fight at all."

"No," laughed the king, "one man against my entire army isn't fair at all, is it? Let's call a truce. I'm going to have to accept this man as my future son-in-law."

The princess and the prince were utterly delighted. They spent a day celebrating the engagement, and then the prince asked the king whether he could take the princess home with him and present her to his own family. "Of course," agreed the king.

The happy couple climbed on the back of the flying horse and took off into the sky. "I wish to go home," the prince told the horse, and it swept them away, over the snow-capped purple mountains, across the golden desert and the sparkling sea to the prince's own city.

Suddenly nervous about introducing his new bride to his father, the prince landed in the royal gardens a little way from the palace. "Would you mind waiting here for me," he asked, "so that I can tell my family you're coming and we can have a proper procession to introduce you?"

"Anything you wish, my love," the princess said happily. So she sat in the gardens and waited with the flying horse while the prince went to announce their arrival.

When the prince got to the palace, his father ran out to greet him with tears of happiness in his eyes. "I thought you were gone forever!" he cried.

"I'm sorry, Father," said the prince. "I got a little carried away and have so much to tell you. First things first, where is the sorcerer who made the flying horse? I must see that he is rewarded!"

"I'm afraid I threw him into the dungeon," admitted the king, and he summoned the guards to bring the sorcerer right away.

The sorcerer appeared, squinting in the light and frowning bitterly. The prince apologized profusely for what had happened and awarded him several coffers of gold and precious jewels.

"The best thing about your flying horse," the prince said, "is that it took me to find my one true love. The princess is waiting in the royal gardens for me now."

"She's waiting there now?" cried the king. He clapped his hands and ordered a banquet to be prepared, called his daughters to get ready, and instructed the footmen to bring a carriage to pick up the princess.

In all the commotion, the sorcerer, who was furious about being locked up, and not at all grateful for his treasure, slipped away to the gardens. He found the princess waiting patiently, along with the flying horse. "I've been sent to meet you," he told her. "They are all waiting for you at the palace."

The princess jumped up eagerly.

"We'll fly there," said the sorcerer. He climbed onto the horse and the princess climbed on behind him.

As they flew up into the sky, the princess saw the palace beneath them. But then the horse veered in the other direction and before she knew it, they were flying away across the sparkling sea. "Where are you taking me?" she shouted in alarm. "We're going the wrong way!"

The sorcerer threw his head back and laughed. "This will teach them a lesson."

Far, far away they flew, until they reached the Land of Rum. There the sorcerer made the horse land in a forest, by a stream where they could quench their thirst and rest. He held the princess tightly by the wrist so she could not run away.

"You won't get away with this, you scoundrel," she yelled. But the sorcerer just laughed at her.

Suddenly they heard the sound of hooves and five men rode out of the trees. The man in front wore a golden crown, and as soon as he saw the beautiful princess, his face lit up with a smile. He said, "I am the King of Rum. What are you doing in my forest?"

"I am a weary voyager," said the sorcerer, "and this is my niece–"

"I'm nothing of the kind," interrupted the princess. "I'm a princess who has been kidnapped by this horrible man, and I demand that he release me immediately."

"Seize him, and throw him in my dungeon," ordered the king, and at once four men leaped forward and took hold of the sorcerer. The king glanced at the horse, "And bring this lovely statue with us too." To the princess, he said, "May I offer you a ride to my palace?"

The princess accepted the king's offer, and away they rode. He had taken a liking to her, so he invited her to dinner. While they ate, she told him her story. "So you see, I really must get back to my prince. I'd be grateful for any help you can offer," she finished.

The king's smile faded a little when he learned of the prince. "It will be difficult to find him, not knowing where he comes from," he said. "But of course I'll do my best, but for now you must stay here with me."

The princess stayed at the palace that day, and the next, and the following day. Each day the king took her riding, or held a ball for her, or gave her beautiful gifts in a vain attempt to make her love him. Every day the princess asked for news of her beloved prince. "Nothing yet," the king would reply. And so the days went by.

As for the prince, as soon as he had discovered the princess was missing, and realized that the sorcerer must have taken her, he set out to find her. He went from town to town, and country to country, asking people if they had seen her, and looking for clues.

Eventually he appeared in the Land of Rum, where he overheard one merchant telling another about the king having found a beautiful princess, her kidnapper and a statue of a horse.

The prince's heart was filled with hope, and he was about to rush off to the palace, when the merchant continued, "I've heard that the king loves her, but she won't have him and longs for some prince she used to know. She keeps telling him that the horse can fly, but she can't fly it. She's a strange one."

The prince stopped in his tracks, realizing he would have to tread very carefully with this king. He thought of a plan, then went to the palace, disguised as a doctor.

"I wanted to offer my services," he told the king. "I can cure all kinds of things, from lack of love to madness. Once I even cured someone who believed a statue could fly…"

The king was about to wave him away, but he pricked up his ears when he heard this. "Perhaps you can help me after all," he said. He told the prince all about the princess. "She has no reason not to love me," he said. "And yet she does not. Also, she keeps talking about this statue of a horse that can fly. All my wisest advisors have attempted to fly it, but of course it doesn't really fly at all."

The prince shook his head gravely. "I can cure her of this delusion," he said. "But you need to bring her and the statue to me."

The princess was brought before the prince. Her eyes lit up as she recognized him, but when he frowned at her, she realized he was planning something. So she kept quiet and pretended not to know him.

"The king tells me you believe this horse can fly," said the prince gravely.

The princess nodded. "It *can* fly," she replied.

"I am here to prove to you that it can't," he said. He got on the horse. "Please mount the horse with me," he said.

The king helped the princess into the saddle, and then stood back. To his dismay, the horse rose immediately into the air.

"It seems you were wrong. This horse can fly after all," the prince called down. "You should have believed the princess. You were wrong about another thing too. You cannot force someone to love you. Love is a thing given by choice. This princess has given me her love, and I have given her mine. I hope you find your own true love one day too. Goodbye!"

The prince took the princess back home with him. A week later, her father and half of her kingdom joined them to celebrate the happiest wedding ever known. For their honeymoon, the happy couple rode all around the world on the magical flying horse.

Sheherazade finished the story and fell silent. "That story was amazing!" said the sultan. Sheherazade smiled. "That's nothing compared to the story I can tell you tomorrow," she said, "as long as you let me live."

"Very well," said the sultan, "I will spare your life for one more day."

The next night,
when the sultan was settled in his bed,
Sheherazade began...

The Poor Man's Dream

nce there was a poor man who had a dream. In his dream, a golden genie appeared and said, "Go to Cairo to seek your fortune. You will return home a rich and happy man."

As soon as he awoke the next morning, the poor man packed a bag and set out on his donkey to Cairo. It took him weeks to get there. On the way he drank from streams, ate dates and apricots from the trees, and slept on the ground beneath the stars.

When he arrived in Cairo, it was late. He couldn't afford to stay in an inn, so he tied up his donkey outside the mosque, and crept inside to sleep there.

In the dead of night a noise woke him up. He went outside to see what had caused it. There he found a band of robbers breaking into the house next door. They had forced open the door and were sneaking inside.

"Stop, thieves!" the poor man shouted. The robbers fled immediately, leaving the man

alone in the street, standing outside the house
with the broken door.

People came running from down the street.
They seized the poor man, and shouted at him,
"You rotten thief. Would you steal from our
friend's house when he is not at home?"

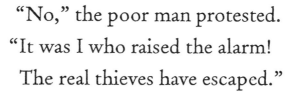

"No," the poor man protested.
"It was I who raised the alarm!
The real thieves have escaped."

"Do you think we believe
that?" said the man who held him
by the scruff of the neck. "We'll
see about this. You ought to be
locked up."

And the poor man was dragged
away and presented to the chief of police.

"I'll take it from here," said the chief of police.

"You should all go home to your beds." When the crowd had gone, the chief of police started questioning the poor man.

"Where did you come from?" he demanded.

"Baghdad," answered the poor man.

"And why did you come to Cairo?" asked the chief of police.

"Because of my dream," the poor man told him miserably.

"What dream?" asked the chief of police.

The poor man explained: "I had a dream in which a genie told me I should go to Cairo and seek my fortune. He said I would return home a rich and happy man," he said. "But all I have found here so far is a terrible night's sleep, an unfair accusation, and trouble with the police. I'm a very *un*happy man."

The chief of police burst out laughing. "You are a fool to take notice of a nonsense dream," he said. "I had a dream too. In fact, I had it three times in a row. I was told to go to Baghdad and find a cobbled street lined with palm trees. In a shabby, blue house on a corner, I would find my fortune. The house belongs to a poor man, but if I dug a hole in its courtyard, I would find riches beyond compare. What utter nonsense! Do you think I rushed off to Baghdad when I had this dream? Of course not!"

The chief of police was so amused he let the poor man go. "Go home," he said. "And don't let me catch you here again."

The poor man retrieved his donkey and went home to Baghdad. He arrived at his street grinning from ear to ear. It was a cobbled street

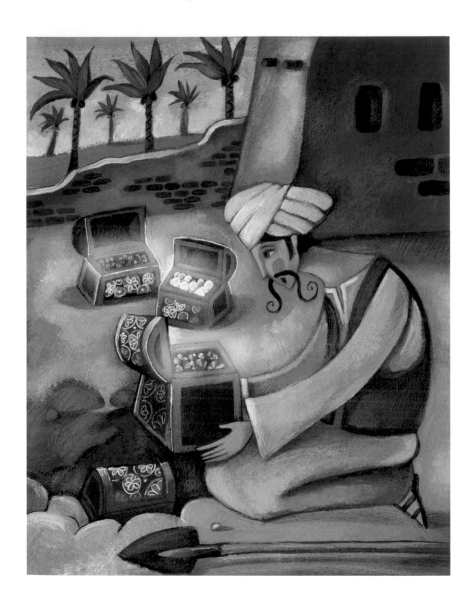

lined with palm trees, and his house was a shabby, blue one on the corner, just like the one in the chief of police's dream.

The poor man went into his courtyard and dug a hole. There in the ground he found riches beyond compare. He pulled up chest after chest of gold, sapphires, rubies and pearls.

He was never, ever poor again, and lived the rest of his days in happiness and comfort.

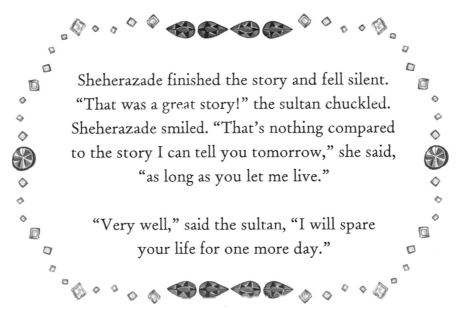

Sheherazade finished the story and fell silent. "That was a great story!" the sultan chuckled. Sheherazade smiled. "That's nothing compared to the story I can tell you tomorrow," she said, "as long as you let me live."

"Very well," said the sultan, "I will spare your life for one more day."

The next night,
when the sultan was settled in his bed,
Sheherazade began…

The Voyages of Sindbad the Sailor

One hot summer's day, a poor porter named Sindbad was struggling along with a heavy burden, when he came to a bench in the shade. He sat down to rest and noticed a beautiful gate in the wall next to him.

Wonderful music and enticing perfumes drifted out from the gate, and he could hear a murmur of happily chattering voices.

Sindbad sighed, and then sang himself a song:

Men are all born just the same,
But their lives are different as can be.
Some get to rest in comfort,
Some have to work like me.

He was just about to continue on his way, when a young boy came out of the gate. The boy bowed and said, "My master sent me to fetch you. Please will you come with me?"

"There must be a mistake," said Sindbad. "I don't belong in a nice place like that."

The boy shook his head. "There's no mistake.

My master asked to meet the man who was singing outside his gate."

"Oh dear," thought Sindbad, "I hope he isn't going to be angry with me for what I sang..." He followed the boy through the gates.

Sindbad the porter had never seen anywhere as lovely as the courtyard inside. It was full of exotic plants with trailing leaves and pretty, scented flowers. Birds of every kind perched on the branches and sang. In the middle, an ornate fountain splashed, and musicians were playing gentle music.

The boy led Sindbad to a low table, surrounded by well-dressed men all sitting on embroidered cushions. At the head of the table sat a man with white streaks in his beard.

"Welcome!" he said. "I liked your song.

I wondered if you might sing it again for us?"

Sindbad was embarrassed. Still, he cleared his throat and sang his song again. This time he added another little verse:

Still I'm not complaining,
I know God has a plan,
For poor Sindbad the porter,
As well as the next man.

"Bravo!" cried his host when he'd finished. "What a coincidence that your name is Sindbad – that's my name! I'm Sindbad the sailor. Perhaps we were meant to meet like this. Please join me and have something to eat and drink."

Sindbad the porter couldn't believe his luck. He sat down at the table and helped himself to the delicious food and drink.

In the meantime, his host said, "It's very pleasant to sit here in comfort and chat to guests. But I have to tell you, I've had my fair share of difficulty getting here. I have made seven voyages in my life, each one more extraordinary than the last. Would you like to hear about them?"

"Yes please," said Sindbad the porter. The other guests nodded eagerly.

"Then I'll begin," said Sindbad the sailor...

Voyage 1
The Disappearing Island

When I was young, my father died, leaving me all his money. I lived comfortably for a long time. But one day I realized that the money was nearly all gone, and I had nothing to show for it. I said to myself, "So far I've done nothing but spend my father's money. What a dull life! I think I'll find a job and go in search of some adventure."

That very day I sold everything I had left, bought some fine pieces of silk, and went down to the port. I found a merchant's ship destined for foreign lands, paid the captain and got on board.

There were six other merchants on board along with me. We sailed across the sea, stopping at every port we found to sell our goods and buy more things to sell. I enjoyed this life – meeting new people all the time, and seeing new places.

We sailed further and further from home, and for a whole week we saw no land at all. Then, one morning, we came to an island in the middle of the calm blue sea. It was a strange-looking island – a big, black hill with a few palm trees perched on it, and a dusting of sand on the shore.

We decided to land, so the captain dropped the anchor, and we rowed ashore in little boats.

Some of my companions wanted to wash their clothes, so they brought a wooden tub with them from the ship, filled it with water, and started gathering sticks to make a fire. Meanwhile, I went off on my own to explore inland.

I hadn't gone far when, with a lurch, the entire island began to move. I heard the captain shout, "Back to the ship, everyone. Now!"

Everyone scrambled for the boats, but I was the furthest away. As I stumbled behind the others, waves flooded the beach and swallowed it up. Before I knew it, I was knee deep in water. The entire island was sinking into the sea!

The water put out the fire my companions

had lit, and swept their washing tub towards me. I seized the tub, and leaped inside, just as the island disappeared beneath my feet.

Palm trees, the sand, the shore – everything was submerged in an instant. I stared, speechless and confused at the empty sea, and suddenly before me a vast whale's tail, all encrusted with sand, came out of the water. It hovered in the air for a moment and then crashed back down, sending foaming waves out in all directions. I clung to my washing tub for dear life, until the sea calmed again.

It was only then that I realized what had happened. The island had been nothing other than the back of a huge whale! It must have floated on the surface of the sea for so long that trees had grown on it.

When my companions had lit a fire, it had dived down to cool its back in the water. It was the most amazing thing I'd ever seen.

My sense of wonder quickly gave way to utter horror at the sight of my ship in the distance. It was sailing away without me. I yelled and waved, but it was too late. The ship disappeared and I was left alone, bobbing on the open sea in a washing tub.

Various things had been left behind in the water, so I salvaged what I thought I could use. I found a barrel with fresh water in it, and some bits of wood I could use as oars.

For seven days and seven nights I bobbed along, rowing as best I could, and drinking as little water as possible, to make it last. I didn't know if I would ever see land again.

The hot sun beat down on me in the day, and the cold wind blew around me at night, until I felt feverish.

Then, on the seventh night, as I tossed and turned in the darkness wondering what would become of me, my tub suddenly ran aground.

I climbed out onto a beach and fell on my knees. I dug my fingers into the cool, moonlit sand to reassure myself that this was a real island, and not another sleeping whale.

All at once, the night air was pierced with a volley of high-pitched squeals. My blood froze. Then came a snorting and neighing and a wild stamping of hooves. I sat up and peered into the darkness.

There were seven black mares standing on the beach. They tossed their manes and stared

out into the water. As I watched,
seven large white-topped waves rolled
in from the sea.

They plunged towards the shore, and
suddenly I saw that each was a pure white
stallion galloping along on the crest of a wave.

The black mares stamped and whinnied in
excitement. The waves reached the shore and
crashed over their backs. For a moment, the
black mares and the white stallions reared up

together on the beach. Then the white stallions sank back into the sea and disappeared.

No sooner had the stallions gone, than seven men came running onto the beach. They caught the mares and began to lead them away. Just before they disappeared from view, I gathered my senses and ran after them, calling, "Wait! Wait!"

They were very surprised to see me there, but when I explained that I had been shipwrecked, they kindly invited me to come with them. "We can take you to meet our king," one man said.

"You're lucky to have found us," said another. "We only come here once a year, and there's nobody else for miles."

"What were you doing here, and what were those white horses I saw that came in from the sea?" I asked curiously.

"They are sea stallions," the man said. "Our mares are pregnant now with their foals. Every year we bring them back, and every year they give birth to the most magnificent silver foals. They are the fastest creatures we know. They're so fast they can gallop across the sea without sinking."

"Wonders never cease!" I exclaimed.

They took me to their city and introduced me to their king. I told him all about my voyage and my adventures so far, and he gave me food, clothes and some money.

"What will you do now?" he asked.

"What I want more than anything is to go home to Baghdad," I told him.

"Where?" he said. He'd never heard of my city. He didn't know my country, nor had he ever heard of any of the surrounding places I named.

I slept at the palace, and the next day I wandered down to the port to see if any of the sailors knew how I could get home. Not one of the sailors or merchants I met had ever heard of my country.

But all at once a ship sailed into port that caught my eye. It seemed familiar. The men on board began to unload goods to sell in the marketplace. There were spices and herbs, and some beautiful silks that I recognized. "Hold on," I said to the man unloading them. "These are mine!"

The man shook his head sadly. "They can't be," he said. "They belong to a merchant who drowned at sea."

"Was his name Sindbad?" I asked.

The man's eyes grew wide.

"Take a closer look," I said. "I didn't drown at sea. I'm right here in front of you."

"Sindbad," he crowed. "It's really you!"

I was so happy, I took some of my best silks and gave them to the king and the men from the beach in thanks for their kindness to me. The rest I sold in the marketplace.

The king invited us all for dinner. He and his family listened avidly to the stories of our travels and out homelands, and offered us beds for the night. The next morning they loaded us with lots of presents to take home. We sailed that very day.

It was a long voyage home, on which I saw many strange and wonderful things – islands with mountains so huge they touched the sky, schools of silver dolphins and miniature horses floating beneath the water. But the sight of my homeland was the most wonderful one of all.

I vowed to stay there for the rest of my days. But after a while, I began to long for more adventure. So I started to plan my next voyage...

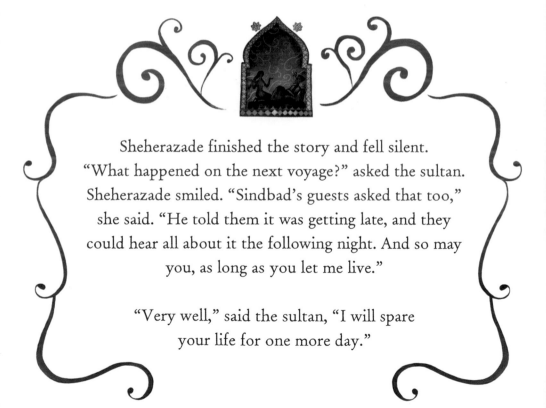

Sheherazade finished the story and fell silent. "What happened on the next voyage?" asked the sultan. Sheherazade smiled. "Sindbad's guests asked that too," she said. "He told them it was getting late, and they could hear all about it the following night. And so may you, as long as you let me live."

"Very well," said the sultan, "I will spare your life for one more day."

The next night, when the sultan was settled
in his bed, Sheherazade began...

Voyage 2
The Mythical Bird

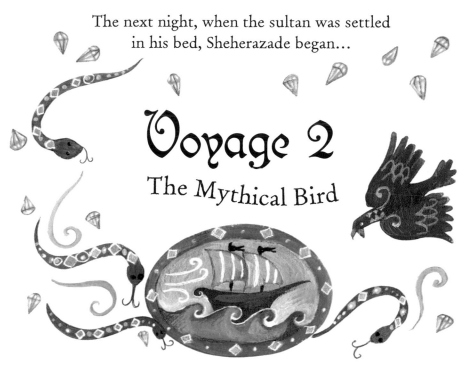

After living quietly for a few years, I began
to long for some adventure. So I bought
some cloth to sell, found a ship and paid the
captain to take me on board.

We sailed away, from port to port and island
to island, further and further from home.

For a whole week we sailed across an empty sea. Then one day we came to an island. The captain dropped anchor, and we all went ashore. It was a beautiful island covered in trees and fragrant flowers. There was a little stream running into the sea, which I decided to follow inland to see what I would find.

Along the banks of the stream grew bushes with soft, orange fruit that flocks of quick, little birds were eating. I gathered the fruit as I walked, and sat down beneath a tree to enjoy it.

The fruit was juicy and delicious. After I'd eaten I felt drowsy, so I lay back in the dappled shade. Very soon, I fell fast asleep.

When I woke, the shadows were long and the light was fading. I'd been asleep for hours. I hurried back to the shore, but it was empty.

I peered out to the horizon, and there was my ship, tiny and golden in the low afternoon sun. It was sailing away without me! I waved and yelled, but it was no use. It was gone for good.

There was no point sitting there feeling sorry for myself, so I decided to climb the tallest tree I could find, and see what I could see.

I did this, and when I poked my head out of the upper branches, I saw the whole island. In the middle, emerging from the treetops, was a huge, white dome. It was vast — bigger than any building I'd ever seen.

"There must be people here!" I thought excitedly. I climbed down and set off to find the dome. Close up, it was even more amazing. The surface was smooth and white with no signs of any brickwork, and the walls were perfectly curved without edges or corners.

"They must be very clever to have built this," I thought to myself. I couldn't see any windows or doors, so I walked around the building to find a way in. I arrived back where I'd started without finding anything. "Could it be that the doorway is hidden, or that there *is* no way in?" I wondered.

Suddenly, everything went dark. I looked up to see a giant shadow in the sky above me, blotting out the sun. It grew bigger and bigger until it filled the entire sky. It was the biggest bird I'd ever seen, and it was coming in to land.

I dived for cover as the bird flew down. Dust billowed up and the trees swayed under its giant flapping wings. The creature landed with its huge scaly feet either side of the white dome, and settled down on top of it.

It glared around for a moment, and I shrank into the shadows, my heart thumping with fear. Without appearing to notice me, the great bird closed its eyes and went to sleep.

I was astounded. As a child I'd heard stories of a mythical bird called a roc that was supposed to be as big as a ship, but I'd never believed them to be true. There I was, standing right next to one, feeling like the tiniest ant next to a vulture.

Of course, the huge white dome that the roc was sitting on wasn't a building, but an egg!

While the creature slept, I thought about

what to do. "It's no use me staying on this island all alone," I reasoned. "It could be years before a ship sails by. This bird must fly to other places. If I could go with it, I might find some way home."

Night had fallen by the time I had decided on a plan. I unwrapped my turban and tied one end around my chest. Creeping up to the bird, I knotted the other end around its thick, scaly leg. Then I sat down and waited.

An ear-splitting screech awoke me at dawn. The bird stood up, flapped its giant wings and took flight. The turban pulled tight around my chest and in a moment I too was airborne. We flew up and up into the sky and out over the sparkling sea. Dangling from the roc's leg, I could see all the way to the horizon. There wasn't a scrap of land in sight.

I began to panic. "This was a stupid idea," I thought. "If it lands in the water, I'll be drowned!" I glanced at the flapping monster above me. I was completely at its mercy. I closed my eyes and prayed for dear life.

Suddenly, the bird let out a piercing cry and began to descend. I opened my eyes to see that we were plummeting toward an island. "I'm going to die," I sobbed. But the roc landed on a sandy slope, and I tumbled down unhurt.

With trembling fingers, I hurriedly untied my turban and scrambled away from the bird. But as I turned, I ran straight into a massive, scaly obstacle. "HISSSSSSSSSSSSSSS," it said. Two cold yellow eyes stared down at me, and a forked tongue flickered in and out of a fearsome set of jaws. I had come face-to-face with a giant snake.

Before I could think what to do, the roc reached over my head, seized the snake in its beak and took flight.

I watched the giant snake writhing in the giant bird's beak as it flew away. Then, breathing a juddering sigh of relief, I looked around to see where I had landed.

I was on a steep, sandy slope leading down into a valley, the bottom of which I couldn't see. There was no vegetation anywhere, only sand and rocks. All around me towered sheer, craggy mountains that no man could ever climb.

"I'd have been better off staying where there was food and water," I sighed. There was no other way to go but further down into the valley, so down I went, trudging through the stones to see what I could find.

As I walked, I noticed a strange glow coming from the bottom of the valley. When I went a little further, I saw what it was coming from.

The valley floor was littered with diamonds. They glittered and sparkled in the sunlight. There were so many, and they shone so brightly I could barely look. I wanted to run to them, but stopped in my tracks. Slithering over the gems were more giant snakes than I could count.

"I can't go up and I can't go down," I said to myself. "What am I to do now?" I sat down on a large rock to think.

As I watched, I realized that the snakes were disappearing into various dark caves and crevices in the sides of the valley. "They don't like sunlight," I realized. When they had all found hiding places, I crept down onto the valley floor.

The diamonds crunched under my feet and sparkled bright white with twinkling rainbows in them. It was the most beautiful sight. I knelt down, dug my hands into them and let them trickle through my fingers.

"I may never get out of here alive," I thought, "but you never know…" and so I filled all my pockets with the precious gems.

The sun was hot, and I was hungry and thirsty. In one of my pockets, I found some fruit from the previous island, which I devoured.

Then I began to search for a way out of the steep valley. I walked carefully around the edges of it, peering into dark caves. But each one contained a giant snake, whose sleeping hisses made my hair stand on end. I had to find a way out by nightfall somehow, or I was sure to die.

Several hours passed, and eventually I flung myself down on the diamonds in despair. But as I lay there, gazing hopelessly at the twinkling stones, something landed with a thump right next to me. I looked up to see a huge hunk of meat, the size of a whole sheep, lying there.

I scrambled to my feet as another hunk of meat landed, and looked up to see more being hurled into the valley from the mountains above. Whatever could it mean?

Then suddenly cries filled the air, and many giant eagles and vultures appeared in the sky above me. They weren't as big as the roc, but they were certainly larger by far than any ordinary birds.

One by one, the giant eagles began to dive into the valley. They seized the pieces of meat in their talons, and flew up again with them. As they grasped the meat, they took with them talons full of sparkling gems.

They flew over the clifftops, and loud claps of gunfire sounded. In fright, the birds dropped the meat and the diamonds on the clifftops and flew away. But they soon returned to the valley for more meat.

Seizing my chance, I bound the end of my turban around one of the chunks of meat, tied the other end around my chest, and waited.

Soon enough, a terrifying giant eagle swooped towards me, seized the meat in its talons and flew up again. The cloth pulled tight around my chest and I was launched into the air.

As I swung up above the clifftops, I could see a group of men waiting with guns. When the

men fired their guns, the eagle above me shrieked
and let go of the meat. Along with the meat and a
shower of diamonds, I plummeted down to the
ground, landing with a thump that knocked the
wind out of me.

The men came to gather the diamonds. They
were so shocked to see me that they fell over one
another. "Where did you come from?" one asked.

"It's a long story," I wheezed.

"Why don't you come home with us?" suggested another. "You can tell us then."

So later, in their little village up in the mountains, I told them everything. They all agreed it was the best story they'd ever heard.

In the morning, I made my way to the nearest port. I asked around among the sailors, but nobody had ever heard of my homeland. So, with one of my diamonds, I bought a ship and paid for a captain and crew to help me find my way home.

It was a long voyage, on which I saw many strange and wonderful things – flying fish with funny faces, islands full of giant trees, and golden birds flying under the water. But the sight of my homeland was the most wonderful one of all.

I vowed to stay there for the rest of my days. But after a while, I began to long for more adventure. So I started to plan my next voyage...

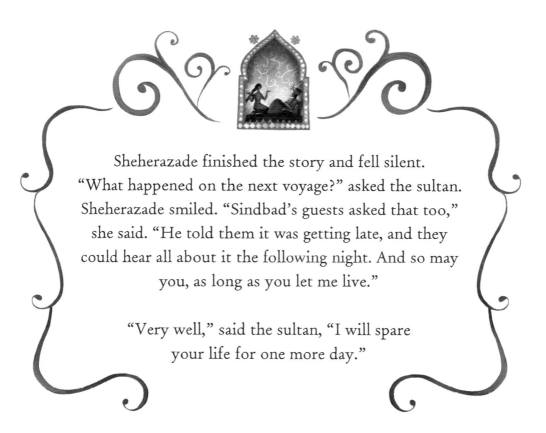

Sheherazade finished the story and fell silent. "What happened on the next voyage?" asked the sultan. Sheherazade smiled. "Sindbad's guests asked that too," she said. "He told them it was getting late, and they could hear all about it the following night. And so may you, as long as you let me live."

"Very well," said the sultan, "I will spare your life for one more day."

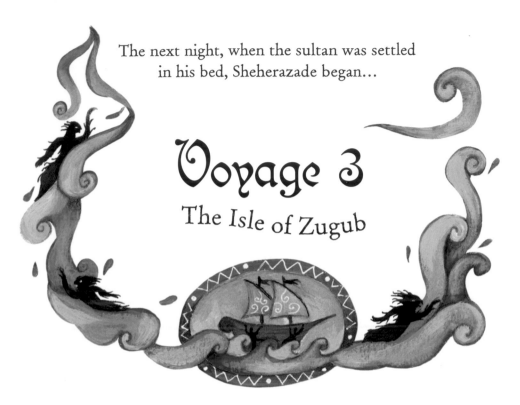

The next night, when the sultan was settled
in his bed, Sheherazade began…

Voyage 3
The Isle of Zugub

After living quietly for a few years, I began to long for some adventure. So I bought some cloth to sell, found a ship and paid the captain to take me on board.

We sailed away, from port to port and island to island, further and further away from home.

One day, we were approaching an island covered in trees, when the captain let out a wail. "We've been blown off course! All is lost!"

"What ever do you mean?" I said.

"It's the Isle of Zugub," the captain wept. "Nobody escapes from there alive."

"Then turn the ship around!" I said.

"Too late," the captain replied. He pointed at the water. Hundreds of black, hairy creatures were swimming towards us. Before we could lift a finger, they were scaling the sides of the ship and climbing on board.

More and more of the creatures swarmed onto the ship and surrounded us. They had bright yellow eyes and tiny, razor-sharp teeth. Hissing menacingly, they drove us all to the edge of the deck and pushed us, one by one, into the water.

To our astonishment and dismay, they sailed our ship away around the island.

We had no choice but to swim ashore. We sat down, sodden and miserable, on the beach. "What will we do now?" the captain moaned.

"It could be worse," I replied. "We're still alive. We'll explore the island and find food and fresh water, and then come up with a plan."

We wandered along the shoreline until we came across a stream. After drinking our fill, we walked inland and spotted bushes bearing purple berries. Cautiously, I tasted one. "Delicious!" I pronounced. We were all browsing through the bushes picking berries, when someone called out, "Look! A building!"

Through the leaves we glimpsed a palace. It had craggy black towers that glinted in the sun, and when we pushed through the trees to find it, we saw a giant gate. It was wide open.

"Is anybody home?" I called anxiously. Hearing no reply, we crept inside. There was an empty courtyard, with a heap of tree trunks piled up like firewood and a vast fireplace, with a large roasting spit in it. The fireplace was surrounded by huge, soft cushions.

"Let's sit down and wait for the owner to come back," said the captain.

We made ourselves comfortable on the cushions. And then we waited… and waited… and gradually, every last one of us nodded off to sleep.

A great crash awoke us all. It was sunset and the sky was blood red. Towering in the gateway of the palace stood a giant.

He glared at us angrily with eyes as red and fiery as the sun. He was as ugly as he was huge. Long bristly ears draped over his shoulders and his drooping lips hung down his chin, revealing fangs as long and pointed as a lion's.

"I'm sorry for the intrusion," I said.

The giant turned and locked the gate. Then he bent down, picked me up and prodded my ribs with his finger. "Too bony," he said.

He dropped me in a sprawled heap on the floor and picked up one of the other men. "Too thin," he grunted and flung him back down.

He cast his eyes over the other men who were cowering around the fireplace. The captain, who was slightly chubby, pushed another man forward, "Try him," he begged.

But the giant gave the captain a leering grin. Ignoring the offered victim, he reached over and picked up the captain. "Mmm," he said, stuffing him into his mouth.

He chewed thoughtfully, while we quaked in our boots, then he swallowed. "Next one better roasted," he said. Then he lay down on the cushions and began to snore.

We scuttled away to the other side of the courtyard and wept. "We're doomed," sobbed one of the merchants.

"I can't think of a worse way to die than this," wept another.

"Pull yourselves together," I told them. "We have to think of something."

"Let's kill the giant in his sleep," one of the sailors suggested.

"Wait a minute," I said. "The lock on the gate is too high for us to reach, so if we kill the giant we'll have no way of getting out."

"How are we ever going to escape from here alive?" wailed a merchant.

We all froze as the giant shifted in his sleep. He rolled onto his side and continued snoring.

"Shhh!" I whispered. "Don't wake him! I have an idea. But for now, stop panicking. We must build a raft and make some paddles from those logs. Once we do escape, we'll need to get away from the island really quickly."

The merchants crept to the fireplace and

brought over logs of wood, which they lashed together with their shirts to make into a raft. Meanwhile, I sharpened the ends of two tree trunks. When everything was ready, I divided the men into two teams.

Each team lifted a sharpened tree trunk. "On the count of three," I said, "We will run forward and plunge these into the giant's eyes."

"But– but–" the men began fearfully.

"Don't think, just do it," I ordered them. "One, two, three… Go!"

We ran forward with our sharp stakes and, as powerfully as we could, thrust them into the sleeping giant's eyes.

It was horrible. He let out a bellow so loud that it knocked us off our feet and made the palace walls tremble. We scrambled away from him as he blindly grasped around for us, the stakes still sticking out of his eyes.

Eventually he gave up trying to catch us, unbolted the gate and ran out into the dawn shouting, "Help!"

"Grab the raft and run," I told the men.

We stumbled down to the shore and launched our raft hurriedly on the sea. The giant's cries rang out all through the pale morning sky.

The cries seemed to multiply, and we glanced back to see a whole family of giants silhouetted on the clifftops. They hurled rocks into the sea at us, but we paddled as fast as we could until we were beyond reach.

Limp with relief, we collapsed on our backs and drifted out into the open sea. But our difficulties were not yet over.

Through the morning, dark clouds rolled in, the wind picked up, and by noon there was a terrible storm. Our flimsy raft was tossed up and down on the churning waves. The logs rolled apart, and we were all pitched into the sea.

In the howling wind and lashing rain, I clung to a log for dear life. Whipped up by the storm, the water heaved and churned, and I was separated from my companions.

Eventually the waves calmed. The clouds gave way to a clear sky, rosy with the setting sun. I looked around to find myself entirely alone on the wide, empty sea.

Exhausted, I clung to my log all night.

By sunrise, I could barely think straight. But a glance at the horizon made my heart leap with joy. There was a ship in the distance.

I waved and shouted with all my might. To my utter delight, the ship sailed toward me.

When I was hauled on board and saw the captain's friendly face, I nearly fainted with surprise. It was the very same captain I'd sailed with on my second voyage!

When I explained what had happened to me since I'd last seen him, the good man's eyes filled with tears. He was mortified at having left me behind on the roc's island, and vowed to take me home.

It was a long voyage home, during which I saw many strange and wonderful things — floating islands, inkfish that dyed the water red and blue, and sunsets that seemed to set the sea on fire. But the sight of my homeland was the most wonderful one of all.

I vowed to stay there for the rest of my days. But after a while, I began to long for more adventure. So I started to plan my next voyage...

Sheherazade finished the story and fell silent. "What happened on the next voyage?" asked the sultan. Sheherazade smiled. "Sindbad's guests asked that too," she said, "He told them it was getting late, and they could hear all about it the following night. And so may you, as long as you let me live."

"Very well," said the sultan, "I will spare your life for one more day."

The next night, when the sultan was settled
in his bed, Sheherazade began...

Voyage 4
The Cannibal King

After living quietly for a few years, I began
to long for some adventure. So I bought
some cloth to sell, found a ship and paid the
captain to take me on board.

   We sailed away, from port to port and island
to island, further and further away from home.

At first, we were blessed with a fine wind, and sped along on the foamy sea. Then one day a howling gale struck up. Our ship rolled violently from side to side, flinging us around like rag dolls. As the waves grew taller, the captain ordered us to drop anchor and pray for our lives.

All at once, a ferocious gust of wind shredded the sail and snapped the mast as if it were a mere twig. As a mountainous green wave lurched towards us, we clung on to what we could. But when it crashed down on top of us, everything turned green and I was plunged into the sea.

The next thing I knew, I was floating among splintered wood and several other groaning men. The ship had been smashed to smithereens.

All of the survivors swam towards the largest floating piece of wood, a beam from the ship that hadn't been broken. We heaved ourselves on top of it and started to paddle with our hands. All day we paddled until, at dusk, we finally reached land. We stumbled ashore, lay down and fell asleep.

The next morning we awoke, happy that we'd survived and ravenously hungry. We strode inland to see what we could find.

In a sunlit glade, in a valley full of green meadows, we came across a peaceful-looking palace. As we headed towards it, the heavy doors opened and four men emerged. Sleek and silent, and very solemn, they surrounded us and showed us inside.

A king sat inside on a golden throne. He smiled and held out his arms to welcome us.

"We were shipwrecked," blurted one of the men. "We're starving and thirsty and lost."

"Then perhaps you'll join me for a banquet," was the king's smooth reply. He opened the doors to another room, where a long table was laid with mouthwatering food.

My companions hurried in, sat down and began eating right away. But, as famished as I was, I hesitated. Something didn't seem quite right to me, so I sat and watched.

As they ate, my companions seemed to become greedier. They stuffed fistfuls of food into their mouths. They snorted and squealed as they ate… and ate… and ate. Before my very eyes, their appearance began to change. They grew fatter and fatter until they couldn't reach the food with their hands. So they pushed their faces into the serving dishes to gobble up more. In the end, they were almost entirely round.

Their arms and legs poked uselessly out of the sides of their balloon-like bodies. Their eyes had glazed over, and it seemed as if they were in some kind of dream.

"Enough," said the king sharply. I spun around to see that his smile had changed to a nasty leer. He clapped his hands, and his men rushed into the room with sticks. They drove my friends away from the table, and I scurried along too, trying to hide myself among them.

We were herded into a pen outside, where we were left for the night. I cowered among my companions, wretched with fear. When I tried to speak to them, I was horrified to find they didn't understand a word. They stared at me blankly and then lay down and went to sleep as if nothing was wrong. I didn't sleep a wink all night.

The next morning, the king came out to the pen with another man. Licking his lips, he cast an eye over us. Finally he pointed at the fattest man and said, "I'll have that one for lunch."

The man seized the unprotesting victim and led him away. The rest of us were herded out to a field.

When we got there, my companions began rooting around and snuffling in the grass like pigs. I sat down and wept in despair.

I looked up to see the herdsman staring at me, and my heart sank. He beckoned for me to come closer. My knees were trembling and my skin was cold with fear, but I went closer.

He pointed to the brow of the hill and hissed. "Go now, if you want to live. Run that way!"

I nodded, speechless with terror and relief, and ran for my life.

For seven days and seven nights, I ran as fast as I could to get away from that place. I ate whatever berries and roots I could find, and drank from streams I passed. I climbed a stony path through the mountains, scrambling over ridges and leaping across ravines until I finally came to the other side.

The air was clear, the sky was blue, and below me stretched another land. In the distance the sea sparkled like precious jewels.

I decided to head for the coast. Some men were gathering spices in a field below me. As I neared them, my stomach lurched with fear. Were they more cannibals? My legs carried me towards them. I hadn't the heart to turn back.

One of them looked up and smiled kindly, and I was flooded with a giddy sense of relief. "Hello," he said. "What brings you this way?"

I told him, in a rush, where I had been, and the man's face filled with pity. "You poor soul," he said. "I'm afraid it's too late to help your friends, but you must come home with us."

They took me on a boat back to their island, which was a few hours' voyage away. As we drew in to port, I was filled with admiration – the town rose in columns and pillars and domes from the sea into the hills above. They were intricately carved and beautifully built. Here, at last, was a place where I could enjoy myself.

The spice pickers told me, "Every visitor who comes to the island is taken to our king, who makes him welcome. So shall you be."

He paid a young boy a coin and asked him to run up to the palace to announce our arrival. Then my new friends led me through wide streets, busy with throngs of cheerful people pulling carts full of spices, vegetables and exotic fruits, and riding elegant horses.

I noticed that nobody was using a saddle. It seemed odd to me that in such a refined place, everybody should ride bareback.

The palace was the most beautiful building of all, with intricate designs made from tiny, bright tiles – turquoise, ruby red, emerald and saffron pieces were arranged into swirling designs.

The king stood outside surrounded by courtiers, all of whom smiled welcomingly at my approach. He invited our whole group inside to eat with him.

While we dined, I told my story. The king was amazed at everything I had lived through. I told him also that I was impressed with his kingdom, but that one thing puzzled me. "Why is it," I asked, "that nobody uses a saddle to ride a horse?"

The king looked puzzled. "A saddle?" he asked. "I have never heard of such a thing."

I described what a saddle was, and what it looked like. "It's much more comfortable than riding bareback," I added. "I think I could make one for you, if I had the right materials."

The king thought it was a splendid idea. He directed me to the best craftsmen in town, and promised he would pay all the bills for the work.

I made some drawings and spoke to the carpenter, who helped me make a wooden frame. Then I took some leather and stitched it onto the frame. I got the blacksmith to make some stirrups and a weaver to weave a length of cloth, which I used to fasten the stirrups to the saddle. Then I had the saddle embroidered with a rich design fit for a king. Finally, I put the saddle on the king's horse and led it before him.

At first, the king looked at the saddle curiously. Then he mounted his horse and rode it around the grounds of the palace. He came back to me with a smile on his face. "I love it!" he declared.

He rewarded me with
a coffer of rubies, and
ordered me to make
more saddles for all
of his courtiers.
I rented a little
workshop, with a room
above it for sleeping in, and
I set to work.

When the courtiers all had saddles, the richest
ladies and gentlemen of the town paid me to
make some more for them. The payment was
always in gemstones, which was the currency of
the island rather than gold or silver. I made more
and more saddles, and an absolute fortune.

The king invited me to dine with him once a
week, and seemed very pleased with my progress.

I made some friends among his courtiers and got to know the king's niece, who was the sweetest lady I had ever met.

One evening, the king said to me, "Almost everybody on the island has a saddle now. What will you do with your skills when there are no more to be made?"

"I will buy a ship," I said happily, "and pay a crew to sail me home. I like your country and its people. But I've been away too long."

The king's face fell. And, I noticed, his niece looked very sad. "How can we persuade you to stay?" said the king. "Perhaps, if someone had captured your heart, you might consider making a home here."

I closely watched his niece's face. She looked down at her hands and blushed as he spoke.

"Perhaps I could make my home here, if I had also captured someone's heart?" I said cautiously. The lady looked up at me with sparkling eyes, and I knew her answer.

The king had followed my gaze and smiled broadly. "It is settled!" he cried. "You will marry my niece." He joined our hands there and then, with a ceremony that bound us for life.

I tell you, I had never been happier. I was so in love, I thought I would never need to go to sea again. I bought a little house with a wonderful garden, and we lived very happily there for a few months. Then something dreadful happened.

My wife's sister became terribly unwell. She was married to the king's chief advisor, and lived nearby. My wife nursed her, and the doctor gave her medicine, but she grew weaker and weaker and died within a week.

Her husband was devastated. "I never thought my life would end so soon," he said.

I thought this was an odd comment, despite his love for his dead wife. "It is her life that has ended," I said gently, "not yours. It will be hard for a while, but you have a life left to live, and you must try to find the strength to live it."

The man shook his head. "You don't understand," he said. "It's the custom in our land that if a man's wife dies, he is buried along with her. I too must die."

I was so shocked I couldn't say another word.

The funeral was the next day, and everyone I knew attended. We went up to the clifftops, where the tombs were. A large stone was rolled away from the entrance, and the woman's body was lowered into the tomb. After that, a prayer was spoken and her husband was lowered in after her, along with a lamp, all his worldly goods and a bowl of food for his last supper.

His sobbing could be heard as the tombstone was rolled back over the tomb. Everybody looked sad about the loss of his life, but it didn't seem to occur to any of them that things could be any different.

A few days after the funeral, my wife said she felt feverish. She quickly became very unwell. I mopped her brow with cool cloths, made her broth to eat, and called the doctor, who gave her medicine. But before the week was out, my dear wife died.

The next days passed in a haze of grief and, before I knew it, I was being lowered into a tomb on the clifftop after my wife.

As the stone was rolled over the mouth of the tomb, I vowed I would find a way to live. Holding up the single candle I had been given, I looked around.

All the gems I had earned from making saddles had been buried with me, and glimmered in the candlelight. "All that is no good to me, if I cannot escape," I thought.

I prowled around the cave, trying to ignore the skeletons and wrapped bodies that lay all around me. I couldn't find a way out, and all too soon, the flame of my candle sputtered and went out. I was left in complete darkness.

Just as I was falling into despair, I saw a thin ray of light at the far end of the cave. Daylight! I rushed over to it, and scrabbled frantically at the rocks, rolling stones out of the way to see if I could make the tiny hole any bigger. Gradually the hole widened and widened until, eventually, it was big enough for me to climb through.

I thrust my head out of the hole and found myself staring down a sheer cliff face into the foamy sea far, far below. I knew I could never jump that distance and survive. So I climbed back into the cave, hunted among the things people had been buried with, and came up with a plan.

I emptied two barrels of wine, and placed my jewels inside them. Then I sealed them back up again and lashed the two barrels together.

Next, I tied together several lengths of cloth to make a long rope. I secured one end around the barrels, then tied the other end around a large rock inside the tomb.

When everything was ready, I sat down and ate the meal that had been left for me. I wasn't very hungry, sitting there among the dead, but I didn't know how long it would be before

I would find food again.

After saying one last goodbye to my poor dear wife, I pushed the barrels out of the hole. I watched them whistle down and splash into the sea below. Then I climbed down the rope after them.

When I reached the barrels, I untied the rope and bobbed away on the sea. I couldn't get very far on a makeshift raft, but I paddled as best I could with my hands, and kept my eyes peeled for passing ships.

As my luck would have it, a ship came to my rescue on my second day at sea. The crew was amazed to find me in such a desolate place. They hauled me aboard, fed me and gave me clean, dry clothes to wear. When I had recovered, I told them my whole story, and they said it was the best they'd ever heard.

I offered them some of my gemstones for rescuing me, but these good people refused to take them. "To save a man is its own reward," they said. And they promised to take me home.

It was a long voyage, on which I saw many strange and wonderful things – floating meadows full of flowers, mermaids swimming beneath the waves, and shooting stars with trails that lit up the whole sky. But the sight of my homeland was the most wonderful one of all.

I vowed to stay there for the rest of my days. But after a while, I began to long for adventure again. So I started to plan my next voyage…

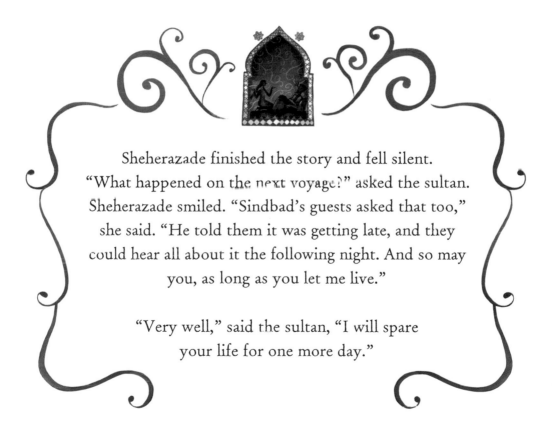

Sheherazade finished the story and fell silent. "What happened on the next voyage?" asked the sultan. Sheherazade smiled. "Sindbad's guests asked that too," she said. "He told them it was getting late, and they could hear all about it the following night. And so may you, as long as you let me live."

"Very well," said the sultan, "I will spare your life for one more day."

The next night, when the sultan was settled
in his bed, Sheherazade began...

Voyage 5
The Old Man of the Sea

I lived in comfort for a few years and forgot all about the horrors of the cannibal king and the clifftop tomb. But eventually, I found myself longing to go back to sea. So, taking money from my coffers, I bought some rich silks, and went down to the port to find a ship.

On the wharf, I noticed a new ship with a gleaming deck, and tall masts with elegant white sails. I bought it there and then, and hired a captain and a crew to sail it. Six other merchants paid passage to come on board.

We set sail on a fine day, with a steady wind, and sailed for many weeks, from port to port and island to island, buying and selling our wares.

Then one day, we came to a small island. We went ashore to rest and gather fruit. Entering a forest, we glimpsed something white between the trees. One of the merchants climbed a tree and called, "It's some kind of dome. Let's go and see whether anybody lives there."

We pushed our way through the dense trees, and came out in a glade where the dome rested. My companions ran around it excitedly, feeling the smooth curved sides with their hands, and shouting, "Where's the door?"

But I knew better. "This is no building," I said. "It's the egg of a gigantic bird called a roc. I met one on my second voyage."

"A bird's egg?" one man snorted. And he picked up a stone and threw it, hard, at the egg. "If it really is a bird's egg, then we should be able to crack it," he said. To my horror, the others started throwing stones at the egg too.

"Stop!" I pleaded with them.

There was a sudden CRACK, and a dark jagged line appeared down the side of the egg.

I was horrified. "When the roc finds its egg broken, it will kill us!" I shouted.

But the merchants just laughed. "It's a bird," one hooted at me. "How ferocious can it be?"

At that very moment, a shadow fell over us as something blotted out the sun. We looked up to see not one, but two rocs flying down to the nest. The men's faces turned white and their eyes grew as wide as dinner plates.

The rocs gave two ear-piercing, angry cries, and everyone clapped their hands over their ears and cowered in terror. "Run for your lives!" I yelled, and scrambled away.

The rocs dived, and the men scattered, running for the cover of the trees. We ran as fast as we could back to the ship, threw ourselves on board and set sail.

We looked back to see the rocs swooping towards us, each with a gigantic stone in its beak. The first one flew high over the ship and let loose a stone the size of an elephant.

The captain swung the tiller and the ship turned sharply, keeling dangerously over to one side. The stone plunged into the water, narrowly missing our stern.

The giant waves it created tipped the ship over so that the deck was almost vertical. Men tumbled helplessly into the sea. "Men overboard!" shouted the captain, desperately trying to right the ship.

Just then, the second roc dropped a stone the size of a house on top of us. It crashed down through the deck, smashing it to splinters. Water glugged into the hold, and the ship began to sink.

Then the first roc dropped a rock the size of a palace through the bow of the sinking ship. I just had time to hear the rocs' triumphant shrieks before I was pulled underwater.

When I surfaced among the wreckage, I found myself alone. Tragically, every other soul had sunk beneath the waves.

I hauled myself onto a couple of splintered planks, fished out two smaller pieces of wood and started to row. Luckily, I soon reached another island. I waded ashore thanking God that my life had been spared.

The island was beautiful, with tropical trees and brightly feathered birds flitting around. I found sparkling streams and fruit trees hung with all kinds of sweet-smelling, red and yellow fruits. I picked and ate all I could.

As I was following a stream on the far side of the island, I turned a corner to find an old man sitting under a tree. I stopped, surprised to find anyone there, and said, "Good day to you, sir."

The man had long, white, hair and a knotted
beard which had seashells and starfish tangled in
it. He stared despondently at the river, but did
not answer me.

"Are you well?" I asked. "Is there any way I
can help you?"

The man squinted up at me, and then nodded.
He pointed across the river, and then to me, and
then himself.

"Would you like me
to carry you across the
river?" I hazarded.

The old man's eyes
lit up and he nodded.
So I lifted him onto
my shoulders and
waded across the river.

He was much heavier than he looked, and he gripped my neck firmly with his legs.

I reached the other side, and kneeled down to put him down, but the old rascal tightened his grip. "What is it now?" I asked.

He kicked my ribs, as though I were a donkey, and pointed to a nearby fruit tree. "You want to pick some fruit? Very well…" I said. I trudged over to the tree. He plucked some of the fruit and bit into it greedily. Juice dripped all over my head and into my hair.

"Do you mind?" I said a little grumpily. I tried again to put him down, but he squeezed his thighs so tightly around my ears that I thought my head would burst. "How long am I supposed to carry you?" I snapped.

Another dig in the ribs urged me forward

through the trees. I trudged around, and the old man picked fruit and munched on it at his leisure.

In the end, I lost patience. "Enough is enough. I'm putting you down now," I said. I crouched down, and tried to push him off, but again he tightened his hold on me, so I could barely breathe. Desperately, I tried to wrench his legs from around my neck, but he squeezed until my head spun. I fell to the ground and passed out.

I came to, and was horrified to find his legs still wrapped firmly around my neck. As soon as he realized I was awake, the old man grunted, and kicked me in the ribs so I would get up.

The whole day, he rode me around the island. He directed me to a field of large, orange gourd fruit with thick skins. He picked one and then directed me to the stream, the bed of which was littered with sharp stones. He pointed to the stones, so I picked up a couple of them. He took one and used it to slice through the skin of the fruit. While he did so, I hid the other stone in my pocket, thinking it might come in useful.

The old man passed me a slice of the fruit. At first I was delighted, thinking he was being kind. But I quickly realized it was more from practicality than kindness. I wouldn't be much good as a means of transport if I fainted from hunger. Still, the fruit was delicious. It was soft and sweet, with pale, crunchy pips. The old man urged me to hurry, grunting irritably as I rushed to finish eating.

By this time the sun was setting. The old man rode me to a forest, where we found a bed of moss to lie on. I lay down with the old man still clinging fast, and wondered miserably whether I would ever be free again.

I didn't sleep a wink that night. As the stars twinkled in the night sky, I racked my tired brains for a plan for my escape.

In the morning we went back to pick more gourd fruit. While the old man was busy eating, I used my stone to slice the top off a gourd and scoop out the flesh. When the old man urged me on, I took the hollowed-out gourd with me.

That evening, while the old man slept, I picked some long grass that was just within my reach and wove it together to make string. Then I poked a hole in the gourd, and tied the string to it.

The following morning, we stopped at some palm trees to pick bananas. Quickly, I tied my gourd to the tree and made a cut in the bark above it. Sap began to seep out of the cut and drip into the gourd.

Two days later, when we passed that way again, I lifted the gourd from the tree and smelled its contents. I grinned broadly to myself. Just as I'd planned, the sap had turned into palm wine.

The old man cuffed me around the head when he saw what I was doing. So I passed the gourd to him. He took a sip, and laughed with glee. He liked it! He tipped his head back and greedily gulped down the whole lot.

Of course, after drinking that much palm wine, he was drunk. He swayed around on my shoulders, singing a raucous song in a language I didn't understand. I staggered around beneath him, trying not to fall.

His song grew more and more slurred, and in the end he slumped over my head and began to snore. Gradually, his legs loosened from around my neck. I laid him carefully on the ground and slipped from his grasp. At last I was free!

Rubbing my aching shoulders, I strolled down to the shore. I sat for a few hours on the beach, staring out at the horizon. Then I saw a white sail. It was a ship heading straight for the island.

The ship dropped anchor and some sailors came ashore to gather fresh water. Joyfully, I ran to greet them. They were very friendly and offered to take me with them.

Only when we were sailing away did I tell them about the old man. "That was the Old Man of the Sea!" exclaimed the captain. "I've heard tales that he's taken a liking to living on land. But, he can't walk, so he rides on anyone foolish or kind enough to go near him until they die of exhaustion. You're lucky to have escaped alive!"

We stopped on another island, and I was told to help the crew gather pebbles from the beach. Then we went inland, where hundreds of monkeys were playing in the trees.

The crew started throwing pebbles at the monkeys. This seemed cruel at first, but soon I understood what they were doing. Chattering angrily, the monkeys hurled coconuts back at the men. Before long, there were mounds of coconuts at our feet.

We gathered them up and sailed to another island port, where a market was taking place. We sold our coconuts and made some money.

I noticed that almost everyone at the market was wearing pearls. They had pearl necklaces and rings, pearl buttons and even pearl-handled shopping baskets. I asked a woman how come everyone was rich enough to own so many pearls.

"Oh, pearls are two a penny here," she replied. "There are so many in shells just off the coast, that we make everything out of them."

That afternoon, I used some money I'd made to buy four sacks full of pearls. With the rest, I paid my passage on a ship to go home.

It was a long voyage, on which I saw many strange and wonderful things – whales spouting rainbows, otters swimming on their backs and flowers blooming in the sea. But the sight of my homeland was the most wonderful one of all.

I vowed to stay there for the rest of my days. But after a while, I began to long for adventure again. So I started to plan my next voyage…

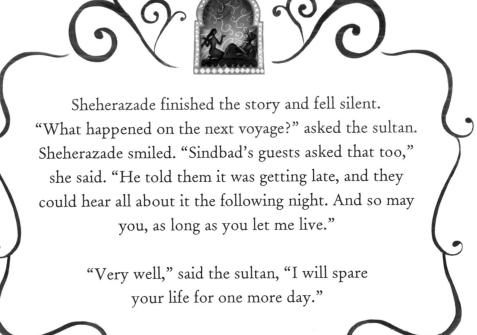

Sheherazade finished the story and fell silent. "What happened on the next voyage?" asked the sultan. Sheherazade smiled. "Sindbad's guests asked that too," she said. "He told them it was getting late, and they could hear all about it the following night. And so may you, as long as you let me live."

"Very well," said the sultan, "I will spare your life for one more day."

The next night, when the sultan was settled
in his bed, Sheherazade began...

Voyage 6
The Land of Jewels

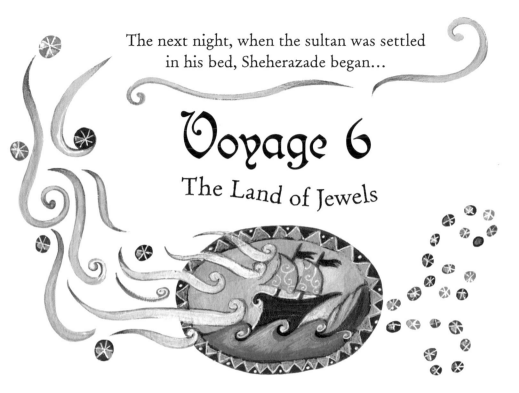

By this time I was a rich man, and had
lived happily at home for a number of
years. One afternoon, however, some merchant
friends paid me a visit. They were full of tales of
a recent voyage to far-off lands. After they left, I
felt a longing to go back to sea...

I bought some silk and a ship, employed a captain and a crew, took on board some other merchants, and set sail. For a few weeks we sailed happily from port to port and island to island, buying and selling our wares.

Then one day, when the sea was as still as a mirror, a ferocious blast of wind came from nowhere. It blew us all off our feet and pinned us to the deck. Filling the sail, the wind pushed the ship along at a breathless rate.

We lay there, our bodies pressed flat as if under some giant's fist, powerless to do anything about it. Faster and faster, the ship raced across the sea. Then, before we knew what was happening, it ran aground.

Jagged rocks pushed through the deck, and the ship keeled over. Everyone slid into a tangled

heap on one side of the deck. Just as suddenly as it had come, the wind died away. Our ears rang with the sudden silence as we struggled to our feet to peer over the edge of the wrecked ship.

We were on a rocky shore, littered with the remains of other ships. Shredded sails and broken masts, splintered barrels and rusty anchors, and other bits and pieces were scattered all around.

As we climbed onto the rocks, we saw that there were skeletons too – the sun-bleached, bare bones of sailors who had been shipwrecked here before us.

"That's what will happen to us," the captain remarked grimly.

"Not if we do something about it," I said, sounding braver than I felt.

We only had enough food and water to last a week, so we searched the shoreline for streams, and sources of food. There was nothing.

"We could fish for food," I suggested, "but fresh water is more of a problem." There wasn't a cloud in sight, and it didn't look as though it ever rained on this island. Dusty rocks rose up into bare mountains, and there were no plants to be seen. "There must be a spring somewhere," I said hopefully. "Let's search inland."

The men had sat down on the beach near our wrecked ship, and they stared at me gloomily. "A ship might pass by while we're gone," said one.

"One of us can stay while the rest go," I said.

"We haven't got much food. We should save our energy," said another man.

"But without water, we'll die!" I said. "Captain, will you come?"

The captain shook his head. "If I'm going to die," he said, "I may as well stay with the ship."

I tried to reason with them, but not a single man would move from the shore. So, taking my share of food and water, and some empty water bottles, I set off alone into the mountains.

For days, I walked, sleeping wherever I stopped at night. I ate and drank tiny amounts to make my provisions last as long as possible. On the eighth day, I swallowed the last drop from my water bottle. I knew I could only stay alive for another day or two without water.

The day was scorching, and I walked at a snail's pace, my throat parched with thirst. At noon, I crept into the shadow of a large rock and closed my eyes. It was so quiet I could hear myself breathing.

Gradually, I noticed another sound in the air: "Shhhhh…" It was just lulling me to sleep, when I realized what it was – running water!

After scrambling across a rocky slope, I saw it: a huge, sparkling waterfall. The water glittered like a shower of gems, and the mist around it was full of rainbows. Never had I found anything so precious. Water!

I cupped my hands in the thundering shower, and held them to my lips. The water was sweet and cool, and I felt life flood back into me. I drank and drank until I could drink no more.

Only after quenching my thirst, did I notice how unusual the waterfall was. Instead of flowing into a pool or a river, the water plunged into a chasm and disappeared underground.

In addition to this, the banks all around the waterfall were covered in twinkling emeralds, rubies, and sapphires.

I was more concerned for my companions on the beach than for the treasure. So I filled the bottles I'd brought and started walking back.

It took me a few days to get back to them. I ran onto the beach calling, "Water! I found water!" But there was no reply.

I don't like to remember the sight that lay before me. All my companions, every last one, lay dead on the shore. I can only suppose they died of thirst. Heartbroken with grief, I buried them there on the sand. Then, weak with hunger and exhaustion, I collapsed.

I awoke in the first light of dawn, determined not to meet the same fate. I found some stale ship's biscuits and chewed on them while I wondered what to do.

There was no hope of a ship coming to my rescue. If a ship came anywhere near, it would be wrecked on the shore like all the others. My only hope was to follow the waterfall underground. It was a reckless idea, but I was desperate, and it was the only plan I had.

Taking the water bottles along with some rope, sacks, a knife, and the last few ship's biscuits, I trekked back to the waterfall.

When I got there, I hacked branches off a nearby tree and tied them together to make a raft. I filled the sacks with jewels from around the waterfall and tied them to the raft. Then, murmuring a prayer, I lifted up my raft and leaped into the waterfall.

The water roared around me as I fell into the pitch-black chasm. I felt myself plunge into icy water. I burst out of the surface and scrambled onto my raft as the current swept me downstream. Clinging on for dear life, I stared, unseeing, into the darkness.

My raft began to bump against the sides of the tunnel, and my turban brushed on the roof.

It was becoming narrower. Quickly the roof and sides of the tunnel closed in on me — I crouched lower and lower until I had to lie flat on my belly. I prayed the tunnel wouldn't come to a dead end.

I felt a lurch as the water dropped away from beneath my raft. I clung to the ropes as I plummeted down and down in the dark.

Suddenly there was blinding light all around me. I was out in the open, falling past a cliff face, surrounded by fine, white spray. Still clinging to my raft, I was plunged once more into cold, deep water. I bobbed to the surface, only to find water hammering down on my head like metal rods.

It happened so fast that it was only then that I realized I had fallen down a waterfall, and was lucky to be alive.

I pushed my raft into the gentle flow of a river and floated downstream. This land was very different to my homeland. On either side of me lay meadows full of spring flowers. There were no trees or shrubs to be seen, only grassland with outcrops of sparkling rocks.

In the distance I could see a city, the domes and rooftops of which sparkled just like all the rocks. When I floated a little closer, I realized why – the stone they were made from was encrusted with jewels. The entire city twinkled with emeralds, sapphires and diamonds.

The river wound its way into the heart of the city. Before I knew it, I was floating under a glittering bridge into the market square. Every inch of every building, even the smallest, was covered in jewels. I was so amazed that I barely noticed the spectacle I was creating.

More and more people gathered along the river to watch me. "Hello!" they called. "Where have you come from?"

The river was wide and slow, and I was able to catch hold of the bank. They pulled me out, along with my raft, handling it with great care. An old man spoke kindly to me, "Come, stranger. Dry yourself by my fire, and I'll give you some food. You look famished."

A couple of men from the crowd carried my raft to the old man's house and placed it gently inside the door. "It's very kind of you," I said, somewhat puzzled by the care they were taking for my battered transport.

Over some warm soup, and wrapped in a blanket, I told the old man all about my travels.

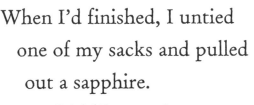

When I'd finished, I untied one of my sacks and pulled out a sapphire.

"I'd like to give you something for your hospitality," I said, handing it to him.

The old man smiled at me, but looked baffled, as though I had offered him a mere pebble.

"Everybody is so wealthy here," I said hesitantly. "It must be a good place to live."

The man looked confused. Glancing at my raft, he said, "None of us is as wealthy as you."

"But you have jewels galore!" I said.

The man shrugged. "Jewels are two a penny here in Sarandib. They have very little worth.

You, on the other hand, have wood. That's extremely rare and precious," he said.

I looked at my battered raft, and then around at the room. Only then did I notice there wasn't a splinter of wood in the place. Dry turf burned in the grate. The table and chairs were carved from stone. The spoon I ate with was metal, as were all the plates and pots.

"Does this country have no trees?" I asked.

The old man shook his head, but his eyes gleamed. "I have heard tell of them, though. Do you know, there are countries where hundreds of trees grow side by side. How rich the people there must be!"

I couldn't help but smile, looking around at his gem-covered house.

"May I make a suggestion?" the old man

asked. "You say you were shipwrecked and left with nothing. But you could get a small fortune for this raft. Shall I help you to sell it?"

"By all means!" I agreed.

By the time we reached the marketplace, word of my arrival had passed through the entire city and crowds of people had come to see me — and, more particularly, my raft.

Several noblemen had gathered in the square too, and when the old man announced that the raft was for sale, they pressed closer. "I'll give you a coffer of gold," shouted one.

I beamed and was about to agree, but the old man put his hand on my arm as if to say, "Wait."

"Two coffers," came another shout.

"Three!"

"Five!"

I was astounded. How could a few pieces of old wood be worth so much to these people?

There was a movement at the back of the crowd, and a commanding voice said. "I will give you twenty coffers of gold for the raft."

The crowd parted to reveal a tall man, who wore a purple robe and a golden crown. Everybody kneeled before him.

"Sold to the king!" the old man declared.

The king came forward to greet me. "I'd also like the pleasure of your company," he said. "You must have an interesting tale to tell."

That night I dined with the king. He asked me all about my journey and about my homeland, and told me all about his. By the end of the evening we were firm friends. "You must miss home," the king observed. "So I'll send you back tomorrow on a fine golden ship loaded with gifts for you and your ruler."

It was a long journey home on which I saw many wonderful and extraordinary things — strange people with wings on their backs, flying fish, and vast herds of cows living under the sea. But the sight of my homeland was the most wonderful one of all.

When I got home to Baghdad, I visited my ruler, the caliph, to deliver his gifts. He was delighted to hear about the King of Sarandib, who valued wood more than emeralds and rubies. "I will send gifts back to him," he declared. "Sindbad, you are the man to take them."

I'd had my fill of adventure, and didn't want to go to sea again. Despite this, I found myself planning my seventh and final voyage...

Sheherazade finished the story and fell silent. "What happened on the next voyage?" asked the sultan. Sheherazade smiled. "Sindbad's guests asked that too," she said. "He told them it was getting late, and they could hear all about it the following night. And so may you, as long as you let me live."

"Very well," said the sultan, "I will spare your life for one more day."

The next night, when the sultan was settled
in his bed, Sheherazade began…

Voyage 7

Elephant Island

When the caliph told me I had to take some gifts to the king I'd met on my previous voyage, I knew I had no choice but to go to sea again. I set sail in the caliph's finest ship. We were blessed with fine winds and calm seas, and reached Sarandib, the Land of Jewels, without any trouble.

The king was delighted to see me again, and so pleased with his gifts that he loaded my ship with yet more riches to take home to the caliph.

Unfortunately, my return journey did not go as smoothly. On the third day at sea, we spotted another ship in the distance.

"Pirates!" shouted the lookout, and we sailed away as fast as we could. But our ship was heavy with treasure and not made for fast sailing. The pirates quickly caught up with us, drew alongside, and boarded our ship.

With glinting cutlasses and rough shouts, they rounded us up in the middle of the ship, and bound us together with rope. Once they had loaded the treasure from our ship onto their own, they led us aboard and threw us in their hold.

We huddled together in the dark all day and all night, sick with fear and wondering what would become of us. In the morning, the ship docked in a busy port. The hatch was flung open and we were dragged, blinking, into the sunlight.

We were taken to a marketplace to be sold as slaves. As we stood there, in shackles, people prodded and poked us, and argued with the pirates about how much we were worth.

An important-looking tribesman wearing carved-tusk necklaces paid a gold coin for me.

He led me to his cart and bundled me into the back of it. The cart bumped along and soon entered a village of mud houses with thatched roofs. As we drove along, everybody stopped and nodded to my new master. I realized that he must be the chief of the village.

We stopped outside the largest hut. My master led me into a courtyard, untied me, and gave me a dish of food and some water. When I had finished eating, he put his face next to mine. "Obey me and I will treat you well," he said. "Defy me and I will kill you."

He locked me in a small hut for the night. The next morning, he unlocked the door and said, "Come." I ate breakfast in the courtyard as he sharpened a set of arrows. "Your job," he told me, "is to kill elephants and bring me their ivory tusks. Have you killed an elephant before?"

I shook my head sadly.

The man noticed my expression. "The elephants are bad. They kill people whenever they have the chance. They come into the village, destroy our houses and even crush our children. We have no choice but to kill them."

He led me through the village and into the forest beyond. Many houses had been flattened, especially those near the forest. Villagers were trying to rebuild them, and I noticed that many people wore necklaces made from carved elephant tusks.

My master led me into the forest and stopped by a very large tree. "Climb this tree," he said. "When an elephant comes, kill it, before it can kill you. Come back to my house at sunset.

Bring me elephant tusks or there will be trouble." My master went back to the village, and I climbed the tree and waited.

The slow crashing of foliage told me that an elephant was coming. Nervously, I raised my bow and arrow, and it appeared.

It was the most magnificent beast I had ever seen. It was a huge bull elephant, with a broad forehead, wide shoulders, and two long, gleaming white tusks. As soon as it came through the trees, it saw me. It glared and let out an angry bellow that shook the leaves from the trees.

I stared down the wavering tip of my arrow at the furious elephant and shook with terror. It could have easily plucked me from the tree like a cherry and crushed me underfoot. "I should kill it now," I thought, "before it kills me." Yet something in its eyes made me hesitate.

Slowly, I lowered the tip of my arrow and waited. The elephant reached into the tree with its trunk and plucked the bow and arrow from my hands. Very deliberately, it snapped them like twigs and threw them on the ground.

Then it curled its trunk around my waist. It lifted me onto its back, and started off through the forest. I sat astride its lumbering, powerful body with my heart pounding, wondering what would happen next.

The elephant gave a deep rumble that felt as if it vibrated through the earth, and an answering rumble came from the depths of the forest. One by one, the rest of the herd appeared and fell in line behind us.

There were about fifteen elephants, along with

a couple of babies with fuzzy heads that flung their short trunks up and squeaked humorously as they trotted along behind their mothers.

Deeper and deeper we went into the forest, until at last we emerged in a sunny glade, where the elephants stopped. I gasped at the sight that lay before me there.

The bare bones of what must have been hundreds of elephants lay in the clearing, arranged neatly side by side, with flowers growing up and around them. The older ones were entwined with ivy; the newer skeletons had fresh flowers arranged around them. This was an elephants' graveyard.

The entire herd of elephants stood in silence looking at their dead relatives. One or two used their trunks to straighten some of the bones and to sweep them clean of dead leaves.

Gazing around the graveyard, I noticed that not a single one of the skeletons still had its tusks. There were several skeletons of smaller elephants too – no bigger than the tiny baby elephants that now huddled under their mothers' bellies.

I suddenly understood the elephants in a different way. They were losing their lives just for the sake of their tusks. All they were doing was fighting back. I had to do something to help stop this bloody war.

I had no idea whether the elephant would understand me, but I spoke to it nevertheless. "I was sent to kill you for your tusks," I began. "I want to tell the people who sent me what I have seen, and tell them to stop attacking you. Will you come with me to show them how peaceful you can be?"

The elephant gave a deep rumble, and began to move. It led the herd through the depths of the forest, past the tree with my broken arrows at its foot, and out into the village.

When the elephants entered the village and marched past the half-rebuilt houses, people fled with terror on their faces. Villagers gathered in

doorways clutching their weapons, but the solemn procession of the entire herd of elephants was impressive enough to ward off any attack.

We stopped outside my master's house. "I have brought the elephant tusks you asked for," I called out. "But I've left them on the elephant."

My master came out. "W— what kind of demon are you, who can tame wild elephants?" he stammered in fear.

"I didn't tame them," I replied. "I think it may have been they who tamed me. Anyway, they have come to show you that there can be peace between man and elephant. They only attack you because you keep slaughtering them for their tusks."

"They are animals," shouted my master indignantly. "They don't reason like that."

"They showed me the elephant graveyard today," I said. "They mourn the loss of their dead, the same as we do."

"How do we know they'll stop harming us if we drop our guard?" came a voice behind me, and I turned to see the villagers gathered in a timid crowd around the elephant herd.

"If you let them leave the village peacefully and stop all violence towards them, they will leave you alone," I said, hoping that this would be true.

"Very well," said my master. "We will try it."

The villagers parted to allow the elephants through. The bull elephant wrapped his trunk around my waist and lifted me down to stand in front of my master.

The great creature nodded his head very slightly to me, then turned and led the other elephants out of the village. The villagers lined the roads to watch, their eyes round with wonder.

My master frowned. "You do not behave like a slave," he told me.

"No man is truly a slave," I replied.

"Since you have talked us out of our livelihood, how do you propose that the village earns money now?" he asked. "We used to sell engraved tusks to merchants who passed by on ships. Now we will have nothing to sell."

I thought for a moment. Then I remembered my previous voyage and the kingdom I had discovered. "I am a merchant by trade, and I happen to know of a land where wood is valued more highly than precious jewels," I said. "You can use your skill at engraving to carve wood into all kinds of things, and sell them to these people. I can even take you there and introduce you to the king, if you'll let me."

After talks with the village elders, my master agreed to travel with me to the Land of Jewels. We went to the port and he paid for our passage on board a ship that was going there.

When the chief tribesman and I arrived, the King of Sarandib welcomed me with open arms.

It was a great surprise to my master to see his slave embraced by a king.

I told the King of Sarandib everything that had happened, and at first he regarded the tribesman angrily. But I explained that I bore no grudge and told him all about my idea. He was very interested.

He and my master discussed the terms and shook hands on the deal. The king would send a fleet of ships in a month's time with payment for the first shipment of wooden carvings. And I was free at last to go home.

My master granted my freedom and we parted as friends. I set out for home, on yet another ship laden with gifts. The journey home was smooth and uneventful, much to my delight.

I'd never been so glad to be home before. I'd had enough adventure to last me the rest of my days. I settled happily at home, and can honestly say I've never felt the need to go to sea again since.

Sindbad the sailor sat back in his chair. "And that was my very last voyage," he said. "When I delivered news of my journey to the caliph, he insisted I tell him the story of all seven voyages."

"Did he enjoy hearing them?" asked Sindbad the porter.

"Oh yes," replied Sindbad the sailor. "He told me they must be preserved for everybody to share, and ordered his scribe to write them down in golden ink. They were kept in the caliph's own library, and have been read by many visitors and retold many times since then."

Sindbad paused a moment, and then he added, "I cannot be sure, but I believe the scribe and tellers of the stories may have added a detail or two of their own... but a story is a story after all; it is there for the teller to tell and the listener to be entertained."

heherazade continued telling stories to the sultan for a thousand and one nights. After she had finished the last story, she said, "I have been your faithful wife for a thousand and one nights, and I've told you stories full of adventure, misfortune, luck, heartbreak and love. Tell me, do you think you can ever love a woman again?"

The sultan looked at Sheherazade tenderly. "Without the shadow of a doubt," he replied. The truth was that he had fallen in love with her a long time ago. "But I have one concern," he said. "Could someone as good, clever and beautiful as you ever love me back, after the terrible things I have done?"

"I already do," said Sheherazade. For she had fallen in love with the sultan too.

From that moment on, the sultan and Sheherazade were the happiest couple that ever lived. The stories Sheherazade had told were retold over and over again, all across the world, until eventually they made their way here.

About the Arabian Nights

The stories in this book are part of a much larger collection of ancient tales known as *The Arabian Nights* or *The Thousand and One Nights*. They don't all come from a single author, nor do they all come from the same place. In fact, how the collection came together over centuries is a tale in itself.

Long before the stories were ever written down, they were told and retold by generations of nomadic people, merchants and voyagers from India, Persia and Arabia, and possibly even from Greece. In the evenings, these people would come together around campfires, or in inns and marketplaces, to entertain one another with stories they'd memorized, of adventure and romance, about everyday life and magical worlds.

The earliest of the tales to be written down – including the story of the clever bride telling stories to prolong her life – probably came from India. They were translated into Persian in the 8th century for a collection called *A Thousand Stories*. No copy survives, so nobody knows which stories were included – or whether there really were a thousand.

This map shows where the Arabian Nights stories came from, and where they are set.

Greece

Constantinople

Syria

Baghdad

'Aladdin and the Magic Lamp' is said to be set further east, in China.

Persia

Cairo

Egypt

India

The main character in 'The Poor Man's Dream' walks from Baghdad to Cairo and back again.

Arabia

Arabian Sea

Sri Lanka

The Land of the Jewels in Sindbad's sixth voyage is sometimes called Sarandib, which is an old Arabic name for Sri Lanka.

Around the year 850, the Persian collection was translated into Arabic, probably in Baghdad. At that time, Baghdad was the biggest and richest city in the world, home to around a million people. It was a hub of learning, culture and trade, with many magnificent mosques, hospitals, schools and libraries.

Scholars came to Baghdad from far and wide to share knowledge and ideas, and to translate and preserve ancient texts in a library known as the House of Wisdom. Its founder, Caliph Harun al-Rashid, appears in fictionalized form as the caliph in *The Voyages of Sindbad the Sailor.*

In the centuries that followed, many new versions of what was now known as *The Thousand and One Nights* were compiled. Just as ancient storytellers would adapt their stories to please different audiences, some of the stories were embellished, and new tales were added along the way, by scribes and translators, mainly from Baghdad, Cairo and Syria. Perhaps they were also trying to make the numbers add up to a thousand and one...

The oldest surviving Arabic copy of *The Thousand and One Nights*, or *Alf Layla wa-Layla* in Arabic, is a three-book manuscript made some time in the 14th century, in Egypt. It contains just 35 stories told over 282 'nights'. Today, it is kept in the National Library in Paris, France, and is often known as the Galland manuscript.

It was from this manuscript, which you can see above, that the first European version of *The Thousand and One Nights* was made, when it was translated into French by a man named Antoine Galland in the early 1700s.

Galland had been posted to the French Embassy in Constantinople (now Istanbul) and worked as an archaeologist in Syria. During his travels, he gained a deep knowledge of the languages, culture and literature of the region.

He had first translated a manuscript of *Sindbad the Sailor* that he found in Constantinople in the 1690s. But he believed this story to be part of a larger collection. Then the Arabic manuscript was sent to him and he began translating it.

Galland was frustrated that there weren't enough stories in the collection to account for a thousand and one nights. He thought there must be a longer manuscript somewhere with more stories. But he couldn't find one.

So Galland split some of the stories into parts instead, so they were told over a thousand and one nights. He also added the Sindbad story, and some more stories that he had been told by a Syrian monk who recited the tales from memory.

Galland's version was published in twelve volumes between 1704 and 1717. These were immediately successful – with adults more than with children, at first. Within a few years, they were translated into several European languages, and adapted for all kinds of different audiences around the world.

Interestingly, two of the stories that are best-known today – *Aladdin and the Magic Lamp* and *Ali Baba and the Forty Thieves* – appeared in Galland's books, but no Arabic manuscript has ever been found of them. It's possible Galland made them up, or perhaps he read them in a manuscript that has been lost.

But if he did add his own stories, it wouldn't be out of keeping with the nature of *The Arabian Nights*. It was, after all, simply a collection of told and retold stories, invented by many different people from many different countries.

Since Galland's time, the stories have influenced the work of many writers, poets, artists and musicians, and been adapted as ballets, plays, movies and even cartoons. In fact these days there are countless different versions of *The Arabian Nights*.

Usborne Quicklinks

For links to websites where you can find out more about
the Arabian Nights, go to the Usborne Quicklinks website
at www.usborne.com/quicklinks and type
in the keywords 'Arabian Nights'.

The recommended websites are regularly reviewed and updated
but, please note, Usborne Publishing is not responsible for the
content of any website other than its own. We recommend that
children are supervised while using the internet.

Edited by Ruth Brocklehurst
Additional designs by Laura Wood
Managing Designer: Nicola Butler; Editorial Director: Jane Chisholm
Digital imaging by Nick Wakeford
With thanks to Peter King for his advice on the stories and their origins.

Every effort has been made to trace the copyright holders of material in this book. If any rights have been omitted,
the publishers offer to rectify this in any subsequent editions following notification. The publishers are grateful to the
following individuals and organizations for permission to reproduce material on the following page:
page 306, Bibliotèque Nationale, Paris (MSS Arabes 3609, 3610 and 3611)